God's Gift

Dana Bell

WolfSinger Publications Security, Colorado

Dedication

First and foremost to God, who inspired me to write this tale.

To the staff of Merchants Mortgage, despite the many interruptions, because they had a hard time comprehending that someone could actually write a book on their lunch break.

For my feline 'children' for teaching me the many interactions cats have with people.

My thanks to Jeff Gerke for showing me you can mix your faith with the speculative genre and Michael Carroll for telling me you can write both secular and Christian. God redeems it all. His wise words aided me during my writing journey.

A special thanks to all the zoos and wildlife refuges I have visited over the years. Watching the lions, tigers, leopards, and other big or small cats helped me craft believable aliens.

I owe a very special thank you to all my fanfiction readers. They know where Lawrence 'Larry' Henry started and gave such positive feedback on him, I decided to take Larry and his family out for a spin in an original novel.

And to Carol Hightshoe, who heard my pitch line at MileHiCon and wanted 'God's Gift'.

Chapter 1

Why does it always rain at funerals like on the holos? Lawrence wondered as he watched the dark cherry casket slowly lowered into the rain soaked ground. Lightning flashed overhead followed by crackling deafening thunder. He saw his sister flinch at the noise and he reached over to gently touch her shoulder. Susanna gave him a grateful smile as tears ran down her pale face.

Not for the first time, he wondered how God could have been so cruel and taken away the only man who had understood his brilliant sister. Gary Gates had loved her and been willing to marry her despite all the traveling her career demanded. Unfortunately, the two had met while she'd been working in London and the rest of the family had not gotten a chance to get to know him very well.

Water dripped over the edge of the black umbrella he held. Larry shook it glad, because of the damp chill, he'd insisted on wearing his woolen uniform rather than the rented dark suit his mother had tried to convince him was better.

"Do not mourn as unbelievers do," the pastor began.

At least this preacher didn't do the usual 'ashes to ashes, dust to dust' speech. Larry guessed the man must be from a list provided by the funeral home since he didn't know him from their regular church.

"Rather remember that we have hope, while others do not,"

Interesting interpretation of Thessalonians Larry thought. Lightning flashed again, thankfully not overhead as before. The rain began to fall harder and boiling thunder rolled over them echoing against the mountains.

The preacher raised his voice to be heard over the rumbling. "Know that we will not go before the dead. Instead, when Christ returns, we who are still alive will be changed and those buried transformed. Forever will we be with the Lord." He closed his Bible. "Comfort each other with these words."

He'd left out many important details in the verses, yet got the gist correct. In all honesty, Larry couldn't fault the man. Maybe he'd hurried the grave side services because of the downpour.

There was a brief moment before everyone began drifting away from the soon to be covered grave. Susanna knelt down tossing a bit of thick mud on the casket. She held out her hand and allowed the rain to wash it clean.

The other guests hurried across the wet grass and crawled into their round domed hovers. Their faces reflected their relief to get out of the storm.

He envied them. His was coming.

"Thank you, for being here, Larry," Susanna said. She looked washed out in black. The color did not compliment her fair complexion.

"You know I'll always be here."

"All I have to do is ask." She kissed his cheek. "I haven't forgotten."

He'd made her that promise when they'd been children. He was her older brother and felt it was his duty to protect her. It had been one of the many reasons he'd joined the Air Force.

A faint rumble, different from the thunder, shook the ground under their feet, followed by a sharp crack. He frowned.

"It's getting worse," Susanna commented before joining their parents at the old fashioned black limo. The wipers were working furiously to keep the front window clear.

Worse? He shuddered. At first, the tremors had been confined to only Wyoming. Now they were spreading. The faint quake they'd just felt confirmed what he'd only been hearing rumors of for weeks in Cheyenne mountain.

"How long do we have, Lord?" he asked, trudging through the soaked grass to join his family.

The four rode in silence back to the Victorian house. His parents lived in what had once been an upscale neighborhood in Colorado Springs. Theirs wasn't rundown like many had become nor overrun with drifters looking for temporary work as they headed south and hopefully, safer location.

Downtown had become much like Denver. The Springs now had high rise towers filled with not just condos, but shops, hospitals, parks, schools, and anything else a person could want. Many living there never saw anything but artificial light. They were born, raised, lived in, died and were cremated without ever stepping outside. Their pretend 'safe lives' saddened Larry.

Of course, some of those living in the mountain weren't any

better. Larry wondered when the idea of isolated lives had become popular and the norm. Some of his college profs, many whose classes he'd taken via the Web, speculated it had started with the advent of personal computers, cell phones, the Internet, and the many inventions complimenting them.

"Larry," his mother's voice interrupted his thoughts. "Coming?"

He nodded and crawled out of the limo, making the brief dash from the street to the protective porch overhang. His youngest sister, Jeanine, gave him a smile as he entered the house. She'd stayed home to greet anyone coming by to offer their condolences or drop off food.

"Glad I didn't go," she commented as the house shook from the storm's fury.

"You never did like to get wet."

"Nope." Her brown eyes lit up as she grinned. "Too much like a cat."

"Speaking of which, where is Leopaldi?"

"Leli is probably hiding under the bed. That's what he usually does."

Leli was his sister's pet name for the orange tabby who had just 'moved in' with his parents. The bedraggled feline had shown up on their front porch and his mother hadn't had the heart to take him to the animal shelter.

"Anyone leave anything good?" Larry carefully removed his uniform jacket and hung it up in the coat closet.

"Always thinkin' with your stomach." Jeanine headed through the archway to the kitchen.

"Why not," he replied as he followed. "Why do you think I joined the Guard?"

"Oh, I don't know." She wrinkled her pug nose at him. "Because you thought the Air Force would be a great place to convert souls."

"Don't tease him, Jeanie," Susanna said as she entered the room. Her eyes scanned the many covered dishes. "At least there's some fruit salad."

"Let me get you a bowl," Jeanine offered, pulling a rose patterned dish from the antique cupboard. "Want a plate, Larry?"

"Sure. Thanks."

The three siblings filled their bowls or plates, grabbed drinks, and retired to the red rose wall-papered dining room. Their parents soon followed and they ate in near silence. Not something they usually did, as Larry recalled.

"What are you going to do now, Susanna?" he asked to break the quiet.

"I've had an offer," his sister answered, pushing aside her partially eaten salad.

"From whom?" Deep in his gut Larry feared it might be somewhere that would take her far, far from home. He reached over trying to tell her silently she needed to stay close to family right now.

She covered his hand with hers. "Classified."

"Always the problem," their father, Lige, spoke up from his normal place at the head of the table. He looked older today, his wrinkles more pronounced, accented by thinning gray hair.

"That's the way it is, Dad." She frowned. "I thought I'd explained that."

"Explained, yes." Their father scowled. "Still ain't right."

"No such word as ain't," Jeanie chimed in.

"You mind your manners, girl."

Their mother, Callie, interrupted before their father went off on the familiar rant about the ill-mannered youth nowadays. "Do you want to take the offer?" Her brown eyes reflected her concern. No doubt she was as worried as Larry was about Susanna leaving her family, just when she really needed them.

"I don't know. They were going to let me take Gary." She caught her breath and rapidly blinked her eyes.

He'd been right about the very far away part. When Susanna had spent a year in Germany, the company who had contracted her had allowed her to take her husband along. Another European company had paid either for her flight or Gary's back and forth to New York every two weeks.

"Do you want to take it?" Larry held his breath afraid of her answer.

"It's the opportunity of a lifetime," she replied, shakily picking up her glass of water and taking a sip.

"You need your family right now," their father said.

"Dad," Larry wanted to stop the tirade he knew was coming. "We can't stop Susanna from living her life." Much as he hated to he added, "If this is a wonderful opportunity, we have no right to stop her."

Susanna gave him a grateful smile while their mother nodded her agreement.

"Always ganging up on me," their father grumped.

"You live in the really olden days, Dad," Jeanine piped up with an impish grin.

"They were better."

Larry shook his head. His father had grown up on a farm in the middle of Kansas, safe from all the violence of first, the Race Riots caused by the rise of Oriental and Hispanic populations producing an abundance of willing low wage workers. The educated working class had rebelled, rioting in the streets and burning government buildings, which had been quelled by force and unfulfilled promises.

The outcome later spawned the Class Wars because the privileged wealthy had no intention of giving up what they thought they were 'entitled' to. Companies had continued to produce only low wage, dead end jobs. Resentful workers had again rioted, storming mansions and killing entire families.

It had taken the election of President Malcolm Smith, a strong, principled Christian leader to stop the violence. Instead of calling out the National Guard, he had forced through legislation, with much opposition from Congress, forcing employers to adhere to what they considered 'archaic' ideas on how to treat workers. The result had been a sudden booming economy and happy, productive workers.

Smith had been called both a visionary and a nut case, yet none could argue with the outcome. He'd been the first of many Christian leaders, pulling the country back to the foundation on which it had been founded and dedicated.

After Smith's re-election, Lige Henry had moved his family from the farming community in Kansas to Colorado Springs. Larry's life had been made easier by what had happened in DC and he was very grateful to their leaders.

What threatened everything which had been accomplished were the quakes creeping farther and farther south and the impending blast from the Yellowstone super volcano. Estimations from the nation's scientists kept changing, but all agreed it could be within just a few years.

And that made Larry wonder how much his sister really knew

about the threat hanging over them all.

"I'm going to go lie down," Susanna announced, pushing back her chair and getting up.

"I put you in your old bedroom," their mother told her. A smile touched the older woman's lips and for just a second, Larry got the image of what Susanna might look like at the same age, with white hair and laugh wrinkles around her mouth and eyes.

"Thanks, Mom," she said. Larry knew Susanna had arrived very early from her latest assignment and probably hadn't had any sleep.

"Has been a long day," Larry agreed, gathering up his dishes and grabbing his sister's as well.

"Learned some things in the military, have ya?" Jeanine teased.

He grimaced remembering his younger days when he'd left all the 'household duties' to the women of the family. "Could say that," he mumbled, going back into the kitchen. He set the dishes in the washer, making a mental note to help his father repaint the room over the weekend, and ambled upstairs to change out of his uniform. Meticulously he put them back on the hanger reminding himself to retrieve the jacket downstairs. Grabbing sweats he threw them on and tucked his feet into an old pair of slippers his mother kept trying to find and throw out.

"You decent?" Susanna called as she knocked.

"Thought you were going to lie down?" He opened the door and leaned on the jamb.

"I am." Nervously she bit her lip. "I have a question for you." He nodded for her continue. She took a deep breath. "You have security clearance right?"

"Mid-level." He wondered why she was asking. "Have to, in order to prepare meals for the brass. That your question?"

His sister gave him a half smile. "No. What I'd like to know," she paused. "If you had your choice of assignments, where would it be?"

"Susanna, I'm lucky to have what I do. Puts me close to my family and my church."

"That wasn't my question."

"Why ask?"

"I've got my reasons."

"I'm perfectly happy with how things worked out."

Her golden brown eyes met his dirt tinged ones. "But if it were possible?"

"God made the decision for me." He'd asked for what he'd really wanted and had been assigned to Cheyenne Mountain instead. Larry had been disappointed at first, yet after being there for awhile and being close to his folks and younger sister, he'd decided God knew best.

"Sometimes, and you taught me this, God makes us wait for what we want."

"I'm fine with how things worked out." He leaned over and kissed Susanna's forehead. "Go lie down, sis. You've had a long day."

She nodded, giving him a curious look before ducking into her old room. He shook his head wondering what she had been talking about. No doubt it had to do with whatever her new offer was, or maybe not. Susanna did at times go off on tangents that were hard to follow—came with the territory of her high IQ.

He closed his bedroom door and grabbed his Bible. The storm rattled overhead and he could hear the rain plopping against his bedroom window. Larry dropped down on his bed and opened to Psalms. He couldn't concentrate on the words. The day's funeral played through his mind and although he hadn't known Gary well, he mourned for his sister's loss.

Dear Father, why?

Chapter 2

Susanna closed her bedroom door and leaned against the thin panel. Her hands were shaking and she felt nauseous despite having eaten. Seemed nothing had settled in her stomach for the past couple of weeks. Maybe she'd drop by a clinic and get something to calm it. She had no doubt it was from all the stress.

Between her husband's sudden death in a fluke hover crash and arguing with his extremely religious parents over the body, her nerves felt as fragile as the crust surrounding a geyser. And thinking about that looming danger, sent her into the small adjoining bathroom to throw up. She tossed cold water on her face afterward and sank down on her old familiar bed.

Tears flooded her eyes and she moaned. The knife like pain stabbing into her broken heart had not lessoned and according to her counselor probably wouldn't for a long, long time. She grabbed the extra pillow on the double bed and curled up with it, venting her sorrow into the lavender scented creases.

Gary, her husband, friend, supporter, lover, and companion, was gone. Dead—because of a manufacturer's failure to issue a recall on a defective part. She remembered the regretful look on the lawyer's face when he'd talked with her and his suggestion of a dollar sum, as if that would replace what she'd truly lost. Susanna couldn't remember the final settlement amount, only that the company had agreed to foot the funeral expenses as well. And she'd made sure it was the most expensive money could buy.

"Susanna?" Jeanine poked her head around the edge of the door. "You've got a call. I told 'em you were lying down, but they said it was important, and…"

"It's okay." She pushed the damp pillow aside and wiped at her eyes. "Mom have any crackers? Lunch didn't stay down."

Her younger sister nodded. "How about I make you some soup?"

"That would be great." They went down the carpeted stairs. Jeanie dashed off to the kitchen and Susanna picked up the cell phone she'd intentionally left there. "Hello?"

"Sorry to bother you, Dr. Gates," the unfamiliar crisp male

voice on the other end said. "But we've had a development and had to move things up. Could you meet us at The Mountain for a briefing?"

"When?"

"As fast as you can get here."

"I need to eat something first."

There was a brief silence. She could hear him talking to someone in the background. "That will be fine," he finally said.

"I'm also going to bring my brother."

"That is not…"

"He has security clearance."

"We're aware of that. The answer is still no."

"I bring my brother or you can find yourself another head scientist for this expedition of yours."

Another silence—longer than the first. "One moment." The man's voice was replaced by a woman's. "Dr. Gates?"

"Yes?"

"Hi, I'm Lin Dragoon, the new leader of the expedition. I understand you'd like to bring your brother."

"I would, yes." She took a deep breath wondering when the change in leadership had occurred. "Look, I don't have time to explain right now, but Larry needs to be there."

"He has the correct security clearance, if the file in front of me is correct."

"He does," she confirmed. One of the many reasons she was being persistent.

"I'll allow it." In the background she heard a couple of raised voices.

"Thank you," she released a relieved breath. It would make matters so much easier. "We'll be there as soon as I've eaten."

"Very good." The line went dead.

Susanna disconnected and decided to convince her brother to drive her since she was both not feeling well and very tired. His protective nature was always easy to manipulate.

~ * ~

The Cheyenne Mountain complex sat high above the Springs where it had for decades, its entrance carved back into solid rock, the arced sign proudly declaring its name. Susanna had only been here once and had not been very impressed with what she'd seen.

The supposedly top secret installation had ceased to be that and almost everyone living in the world knew where it was.

NORAD, which had once been there, had been moved long before she'd even been born and the base abandoned. In recent years, it had been reactivated and several top secret projects, including the one she was part of, had taken up residence.

"Moving out," Larry said, as he maneuvered the hover around the large stack of wooden crates and cardboard boxes piled outside, awaiting trucks to ferry them away.

"Any idea which project?" Susanna hoped the soup and crackers she'd eaten stayed down. Talking helped distract her from her rolling stomach.

"Been on the lake level for years, so, no, I don't really know. What I've heard," he gave her a lopsided grin. "Is that they finally lost funding and had to close up. Most of the personnel have already been reassigned and shipped out."

He drove into the narrow tunnel and parked. Before she could open the door, he turned to her and asked, "Just what are you dragging me into?"

"Remember when you taught the lesson on God and the desires of our heart?"

He nodded. "One of my better sermons."

"Let's just say that maybe, God is making one of yours come true." She got out.

"You're not making any sense."

"I know."

They were met at the big metal door by a bored looking young officer. When presented with their ID he just waved them through.

"How's your mom doing, Tim?" Larry inquired before they went in. He spent a few minutes attaching his badge to his uniform. Susanna waited for him. It was so like his brother to know and care about the lives of others.

The smooth faced kid smiled. He didn't look old enough, even with the buzz haircut, to be in uniform. "Better, sir. Thanks for your prayers."

"Any time."

Once inside Susanna lightly touched her brother's arm. "One of your flock?"

"Hope he will be some day. God has really been working on

Tim's heart."

"I'm still surprised you didn't join up as a chaplain."

"Take care of the physical and it opens a person up to hear the Word."

"Like Jesus feeding the five thousand."

"Yeah." His eyes darted to a sign over a storage closet and hers followed. They both chuckled at the reference to an old TV show they'd both liked as children. In fact, Susanna was fairly sure it was part of what had fueled her brother's still unfilled dream.

"Know where we're going?" Larry wanted to know.

"No. But I suspect this officer is our escort."

The private saluted Larry and smiled at Susanna. "If you'll follow me, please." He led them through the area around old looking computer set ups with military personal crammed behind them, to a small room on the far side. Opening the door he indicated they should enter.

A small oriental woman wearing a silk ebony pant suit rose to greet them. "I'm Lin Dragoon," she introduced herself. "Dr. Gates, Major Henry, welcome."

"Thanks." Susanna warily regarded the other woman, taking in the tall black man standing behind her. He was an imposing figure with his height and crisp tan uniform adorned with colorful ribbons. She had no idea what they all meant. A little intimidated, she asked the first question that came to mind. "I thought Jacob Lane was in charge of this expedition?"

"Change of plans." The male voice attached to the answer was familiar and she recognized it from her earlier phone call. It came from the uniformed man.

"I don't need you to step in," Lin admonished him. "I'm sorry." She pointed to the officer. "This is General Malcolm Borromeo. He's going to be in charge of military operations, and this is," she turned to a seated woman Susanna hadn't noticed. "Dr. Amira Upala, chief medical officer."

The doctor acknowledged her with a warm smile. The young woman wore casual clothes and didn't at all look like she worked in the medical profession.

"And you still want me to be in charge of the scientific team?" With the changes Susanna was seeing, she couldn't be sure if her position was still secure.

"That's correct," Dragoon said. "Though your brother

here—"

She cut the other short. "I told you I had my reasons."

"You did. Yes." The leader sat down, folding her small hands neatly on the plain gray table. "Tell me."

"First," Susanna sat down on the hard chair. Larry settled on the one beside her. "I want you to tell my brother exactly what is going on here."

General Borromeo objected. "He hasn't signed the non- disclosure agreements."

"My brother is a pastor. I think that should be good enough."

"She's right," Lin agreed with a chuckle. "Very well then. If you would, General."

He glared at her but complied. Overhead a large screen descended from the flat gray ceiling. It flickered briefly before a picture appeared. Thin clouds veiled a green, brown and black mottled planet, with a few areas of blue peeking through. In its orbit were five moons.

"In the Talulah system, we've found only one habitable world, Galilahi. No native intelligent life, twenty-five percent water coverage, some active volcanoes, with an average rainfall of about ten inches a year."

"Wait a minute," Larry got to his feet. "What do you mean?" He stopped. Susanna suspected he didn't know exactly what to ask.

"We've been colonizing for the past one hundred years," Lin explained. "Most of the expeditions have consisted of those without families."

Larry nodded as if he suddenly understood. "So they wouldn't be missed."

"That was the idea." She pointed to his chair. "If you'd reseat yourself, I'll try to explain."

Her brother sat back down, throwing a questioning glance at Susanna. She shook her head and squeezed his hand.

"I think you've noticed the drop in the world population," Lin continued.

"Thought that was due to mandatory birth control, strict genetic guidelines, and public education emphasizing caring for our planet rather than exploiting it," her brother said.

Susanna knew how controversial those guidelines had been when first introduced. However, the planet couldn't continue to sustain billions of people, so many countries had adopted them including the United States, despite loud objections.

"That's helped," Lin agreed. "But as you know, we have an even greater threat to our existence."

He nodded. Susanna knew Larry understood. Geologists had been monitoring Yellowstone for a couple hundred years. A decade ago, they'd closed the park to visitors because volcanic activity had made it unsafe. Their actions started the migration of individuals and families south and hopefully out of the predicted blast zone.

"How did we manage to get out into space without the public knowing?" Her brother leaned forward, his large hands resting on the table.

The doctor chuckled. "Pure luck."

The general took over with a quelling look at Dragoon and the doctor. "There was a technological breakthrough."

"Accidental," Dragoon put in.

"Accidental," he conceded, although Susanna didn't miss the odd cheek tick. "We managed to keep it away from the press and confined to the personnel who worked in the mountain."

"So that's why people started living there instead of military housing." She could see her brother's face. His expression was the same when he'd finally figured out how to climb out of the tree by himself at age nine, when most of the neighborhood boys already knew how.

"We thought it safer for all concerned." The general put his hands behind his back.

"How many are still," Larry vaguely waved his hand, "here?"

Dragoon gave the general a warning look. Susanna wondered why. "Only a few. Most have been reassigned to our base in Idaho." She paused. "Where our newest colony ship, the *Namid,* has just been completed."

Susanna started. She had no idea the ship was ready. How soon did they plan to launch?

Chapter 3

Larry understood both why Susanna had kept this to herself, besides it being classified, and why she'd insisted he be included. He appreciated her wanting him to realize his lifelong dream. Yet if this meant what he thought—

"What about the rest of our family?" he demanded.

The leader's face held a sad look. "Your younger sister is more than welcome. Your parents, unfortunately, are over the age limit We need strong healthy adults in their reproductive years."

"And you expect us to leave our parents behind?" The thought angered him.

"I come from a culture that respects our elders. I don't like the idea of leaving my honorable parents behind either."

"We've made arrangements," the general put in, his dark face serious, "with some of our allies to relocate any family members to one of our bases in South America. They'll be safe there from any...fallout."

Understood in one word was the full impact of Yellowstone exploding. Not only would the eruption pour thousands of tons of ash and rock into the atmosphere destroying everything in the blast zone including Colorado Springs, but there would be dramatic climatic changes resulting in crop failures and worldwide famine. Millions would die.

"Oh, God," he groaned in sorrow, his head falling into his hands.

"How long do we have?" He heard his sister ask.

"Six months, maybe less," Dragoon answered. "If you're going to go with us, I need to know now."

"Larry?" His sister's hand touched his shoulder. "What do you want to do?"

"I never wanted to go into space like this."

"I know." She lowered her voice. "I think God has given us a chance to survive what's coming. Sort of like Noah."

"Or Jesus could be returning." He lifted his head to look at Susanna, ignoring everyone else in the room. Larry didn't miss the slight flinch from Dr. Upala.

"But we don't know." Tears dripped from her eyes. "I want to live. I'd like to have at least some of my family with me."

He gathered her into his arms, feeling her body shake with sobs. "Can you give us a minute?"

Dragoon gave a quick nod. She exited the room. The general and doctor followed. Funny, Larry thought to himself, the doctor hadn't said more than a couple of words during the discussion.

"What do we tell our parents?" Larry couldn't believe he was even thinking of joining the expedition.

Susanna shook her head, pulling away and wiping at her eyes. "That we're sending them south for their own good." She gulped. "We ask Jeanie if she wants to stay with us or go with them."

"Leave her here, too?" The idea of their youngest sister staying behind horrified him. What kind of life would she have on a ruined world?

"It's her choice. We owe her that."

"Makes us both sound selfish."

"Mom and dad have always wanted what was best for us, remember?"

He did. They'd allowed him to attend the high school he'd wanted in Denver and then paid for his housing while he'd attended seminary. Susanna had always been encouraged, first through regular school and their parents had assisted her in finding funding for M.I.T. until she finally had her PHD. He knew they'd be willing to do the same for Jeanie. She was in her final year in high school hoping to start college in the fall and dance in the church ministry group. Looked like her future had changed.

All of theirs had.

~ * ~

"What a dump," Jeanie complained as she descended the plane ladder onto the hot asphalt. Her backpack half hung from her shoulder.

"No different from western Colorado," Larry reminded her. He shielded his eyes with his hand and looked over the bleak desert base. Well-kept buildings shimmered in the extreme heat. Young men and women in uniform hurried about the airfield. The three siblings rushed across the short expanse into an air conditioned nondescript building.

"Good to see you," Dragoon greeted, frowning at the pet

carrier Jeanie had. "I thought I made myself clear—" she began. The doctor stood beside her.

"She wouldn't leave Leli behind," her brother quickly defended. "We," how could he explain? His sister deserved to be allowed to keep some part of her past.

"Quite all right," Dr. Upala interceded. "Pets are often considered part of the family. And we've already made a few exceptions."

The expedition leader muttered something in what Larry recognized as Mandarin Chinese. Stiffly she said, "If you'll follow me." She crossed the polished linoleum floor to a set of doors on the other side. "Our group is being housed together in what was the Officer's section."

"I'm surprised there's anyone still here," Susanna commented. Larry wished she'd allow him to carry her overnight bag.

"Only those who need to be here. Everyone else has been transferred south."

Larry noticed her choice of words and hoped everyone here had a place on the ship and no one would be left behind.

"To where our parents went?" Jeanie asked, blinking her eyes rapidly.

"I don't know."

Briefly they suffered the heat again before boarding a large bus driven by a young officer. It bounced across the tarmac. Leopaldi let out a protesting yowl.

"Don't blame him," Susanna sympathized briefly touching her stomach.

"How's the baby?" Larry swung down to sit next to her on the lumpy green seat.

"Fine." She smiled. After her husband's death three months ago, she'd found out she was pregnant. Larry was sure the knowledge had saved her sanity and helped her deal with her grief.

"I've received your records," Dr. Upala said from the seat in front of them. "I understand you're about four months along and it is a girl." Susanna nodded. "That is a good thing. You have a part of your husband with you."

"Yes." His sister smiled. "Gary would have been elated."

"A wise man to value his child." The doctor threw an odd glance at Dragoon who simply looked away. He wondered what that was about.

"Yours will be the first child born on Galilahi."

"Followed we hope," the expedition leader joined the conversation. "By many more."

"Sounds boring." Jeanie reached between the carrier door's metal weaves so her fingers could pet Leli.

"You might not think so," the doctor teased her, "once you get a look of some of those Air Force men."

"You always did like watching the cadets at the Academy," Larry reminded his youngest sister. Then he wished he hadn't. The tears threatening at the edge of her eyes told him he'd said the wrong thing. They'd said good-bye to their parents at the training airfield.

As he remembered, it had been raining. They'd stood near the end of the ramp leading up to the huge cargo plane. The family had been protected from the downpour by the open hatch overhead.

"Hate flying," his father had grumbled, looking uncomfortable in his jeans and red plaid shirt.

His mother patted her husband's arm. "It'll be fine, dear." Suddenly she'd embraced all three children in a hug. "God watch over you," she'd said.

"Mom," Larry had no words. He hadn't wanted to let them go.

Their mother had kissed both girls on the cheek. "I'm so sorry I'll never see my grandchild, nor you in your wedding gown, Jeanie." His youngest sister rolled her eyes. She'd kissed his forehead too. "Nor will I ever meet your future wife."

"We'll see each other in heaven, Mom. God made us that promise."

She'd smiled. "He did." He'd forever have the image of his mother in her yellow print dress, with her short hair nicely done and wearing her favorite brooch.

They'd joined hands and prayed before their parents had vanished inside the large plane as if they'd been swallowed by Jonah's whale. An hour later the three of them had stood inside the terminal, watching the monster aircraft as it rumbled down the runway and into the storm filled sky.

"She needs to cry and express her grief," Susanna quietly said, jerking his mind back to the present.

"Yeah, I know." How many times had that been drilled into

his head during his 'Human Compassion' courses?

"That's what my therapist told me."

"And that's right," he reluctantly agreed. He'd need to grieve their loss as well.

Upala's dark eyes surveyed them both. "At least your sister knows your parents will be safe. That is not the case with everyone."

"Are yours in a danger zone?" Larry sensed the truth.

"I grew up in a small village near a contested zone in Israel. Bombs and bullets were everyday occurrences. My brother is in the military and my parents still live in the same house."

"I constantly pray for peace in Israel."

"I thank you for that." She gave him an odd look. "Are you going to try and convert me to your Christian beliefs?"

"God knows who and who will not believe. Only the Holy Spirit can convict a heart and bring them Jesus. I'd only be a messenger."

The doctor fell silent, her expression thoughtful. "You are a most unusual pastor."

"That's what I keep telling him." Susanna shifted.

Larry didn't blame her. The lumpy seat was hard to sit on.

"We're there," Dragoon told them. She gave them an almost resentful glare before covering it quickly with a smile that didn't reach her eyes.

The bus stopped in front of a small house which looked exactly like all its neighbors. The only difference was the color, a pastel pink-orange shade.

"It only has two bedrooms," the doctor apologized.

"I think we can manage, can't we, Jeanie?" Susanna's face expectantly waited for Jeanine's answer. Larry noticed Jeanie frown before grabbing the carrier and getting off the bus.

"I don't think she's happy about it," Larry commented.

"It's only for a little while."

Brother and sister got off the bus. Dragoon stood on the step but didn't exit. "If you need anything, just call the main office. Number is by the vid phone. House is unlocked and the keys are on the kitchen counter."

"Thank you." Larry grabbed his suitcase and Susanna's. Jeanie had already collected hers and stood by the door.

"I'm very glad you're here. All of you." The Chinese woman

gave a half wave in farewell. "Tomorrow, being Sunday, is a day off for all but the medical team. Monday morning we have a general meeting for everyone."

The ground shook almost knocking Larry and Susanna off their feet. Dropping both suitcases, he grabbed his sister to keep her from falling, His eyes drifted up. In the far distance he could see a plume of black rolling ash rising.

"We're closer here," Dragoon said, following the direction of his gaze.

"Surprised they put the base here." Larry looked at the leader quizzically.

The leader nodded her agreement. "Most everyone except the extreme survivalists somewhere in the pan handle are gone. Our DC sponsors thought this the best place."

"We won't have much time," Susanna observed. He didn't miss her frightened look.

"We'll have enough. I do suggest you don't unpack. We may have to launch without much warning."

Upala slid down the bus window. "I keep my suitcases by the door both day and night or with me at the hospital. That way, they're easy to grab."

"Good idea," Larry agreed, thankful for her suggestion.

"I also stocked your kitchen with some basic supplies, plus vitamins for you, Dr. Gates."

"That was thoughtful, thank you." Susanna trudged up the cracked walkway, carrying her overnight bag." The door's open, Jeanie!"

"Does anyone hold church services?" Larry wanted to know.

"Not right now," Dragoon snapped.

"There is a group who holds a Bible study," Dr, Upala informed him." They meet in the main cafeteria about ten."

The Oriental woman started. "I'll see you Monday." She retook her seat and the ancient vehicle lurched off. Amira waved as she closed her window.

Larry took their suitcases in and glanced around the cottage style house. A few modern conveniences had been added, like the new holo entertainment center and vid phone, but otherwise, from what he could see, the house hadn't changed much from an early twentieth century style he'd studied in school texts.

"Not much to look at," Susanna commented.

"We won't be here long."

"Thank, God!" Jeanie plopped down on the worn brown couch. She leaned down to release the complaining cat from the carrier. "Yeah, I know," she sympathized, rubbing Leli's orange head and turning on the entertainment center. Images flickered quickly as she checked to see what was on.

"I need to lie down." He glanced at Susanna. Her face reflected her fatigue.

He put his suitcase down and followed her to the larger of the two bedrooms. There was a huge king sized bed, an old fashioned dresser, a couple of wobbly night stands, and a very small closet.

"Where do you want me to put these?" he asked her, holding up her suitcase and overnight bag.

"On top of the dresser."

He put the suitcase where she indicated and quickly left. Checking on Jeanie, who had finally settled on a Christian music channel, he trotted into the kitchen to see what they had for food. He opened a faded oak cupboard. There were several cans of soup, more of vegetables and a couple of fruit mixes. Also, he found pudding and Jell-O boxes.

In the fridge there was milk, eggs, butter and several other staples. The freezer revealed some frozen beef and chicken. He shut the door and debated about what to make for dinner. He didn't have much to choose from, but he was sure he could come up with something.

"Wonder if there's any macaroni," he said to himself, opening yet another cupboard.

"Merow," Leli answered. The orange tabby stood on his back legs reaching up with his front paws and putting them against Larry's pant leg.

Larry reached down and rubbed the cat's head. "Bet you're hungry." Jeanie hadn't fed the feline since they'd left home. Leli tended to get motion sickness. "Let's see what we have here."

Chapter 4

Susanna was exhausted. She slipped off her flat sandals and sat on the bed. The mattress wasn't as firm as she liked. With a weary sigh she laid back on the gaudy yellow flowered bedspread, reflecting the room almost reminded her of the many hotels she'd stayed in over the years.

Unlike the hotels there was the familiar noise of Larry opening cupboards and banging pots in the kitchen and the drone of music from the living area. She closed her eyes hoping she could take a nap. The flight from Colorado had been exhausting with bumpy turbulence over the snow covered Rockies. She'd also gotten a much too clear view of the ash and smoke being spewed into the air as they'd landed. She couldn't bear to think what future generations were going to have to endure once Yellowstone blew.

Her fingers settled on her stomach and the new life she carried. "You'll have a good start," she promised her baby.

Tantalizing smells of hamburger drifted into the bedroom. Her brother must have found some promising ingredients. His interest in cooking almost amused her considering he'd once thought of it as 'woman's work'. His stint in the Air Force seemed to have changed his mind. Or maybe God had. More likely it had been the latter.

A loud buzzer sounded and in its wake a piercing yowl. She heard voices coming from the kitchen. Curious, she got up and padded barefoot to join them.

"I didn't mean to wake you," Dr. Upala apologized as Susanna entered the room.

"Wasn't really asleep," she answered.

The doctor's gaze returned to her brother. She held up a bag. "For the cat."

Jeanie squealed. "You brought Leli food?" Her younger sister grabbed the bag and dumped the cans, treats and bagged food on the dingy gray counter.

"If I were you," the doctor continued, "I'd suggest keeping your cat's food with your suitcases by the door. The carrier as well."

She caught her brother's look, an odd mixture of interest and concern. "It's that bad?"

"Most of the basic supplies are already loaded, though most don't know that."

Dishes rattled in the cupboard as ground beneath them rumbled.

"That's happening more and more often," Upala continued. "I overheard Dr. Byer say, he's our chief geologist, Yellowstone is likely to blow sometime in the next week. If not sooner." She glanced at the floor. "I did not say this, of course."

Larry snorted and stirred something in the pan bubbling on the stove. "Would you like to join us for dinner?"

Surprised, Susanna stared at her brother. She could remember very few instances, even in high school, when Larry invited someone to dinner.

"I wouldn't be intruding?"

"Course not." He winked at the doctor. "I'm just looking for an excuse to preach Jesus at you."

Susanna burst out laughing followed by Jeanie. They both knew he'd do nothing of the sort.

"What are you having?" Upala peeked over his shoulder at the pots.

"Just a hamburger casserole with vegetables mixed in."

"Sounds delicious."

"The Air Force travels on its stomach, huh?" Susanna teased.

"Nah, that's the army," he quipped back.

"I'm going to feed Leli." Jeanie opened a can and pulled out a bowl. Her cat followed her around the kitchen, brushing against the teen's legs. "Come on, silly." She took the food and cat to the dining area and set the bowl on the floor. "Call me when it's ready." She flounced out and the volume went up in the living area.

"Anything I can do to help, Larry?" Susanna asked.

"No. Why don't you go back and rest. I've got dinner under control."

'I'll bet you do,' she said to herself. Dr. Upala leaned on the counter, listening to her brother talk about cooking in the military. Susanna went back to the bedroom. She sensed there was more going on in the kitchen than Larry was aware of.

Settling on the bed once again, Susanna closed her eyes and

was soon asleep.

~ * ~

"Leli!" Jeanie called.

Her sister's voice and the sound of the can opener penetrated Susanna's fogged brain as she trudged into the kitchen the next morning, still wearing her clothes from the day before. Larry greeted her with a smile and she settled into a somewhat soft chair.

"Where is that cat?" Jeanine grumbled. "He's been acting weird all morning."

"None of us have been outside, so he's around here some-where." Larry got up and took the teapot off before it whistled. He grabbed a mug, filled it with hot water and put it, plus a tea-bag, in front of Susanna.

"Thanks." Her husband had done the same for her and she had to squeeze back the tears the memory caused.

A shudder rattled the glass dishes and she glanced up in alarm. From somewhere in the house the cat screamed.

"Where are your suitcases?" Larry demanded.

"Mine's by the door." Jeanie put the dish of wet, foul fishy smelling food on the floor.

"My room," Susanna got up and hurried back there. She had the feeling they didn't have much time.

"Hey, look!" Jeanie called. "It's snowing!"

"Find the cat!" Larry ordered.

The floor buckled under Susanna's feet knocking her slightly off balance. Luckily she fell against the bed. Quickly she pulled off her musty smelling clothes and pulled on pants and a top. From the other room she heard the sound of breaking glass and the insistent buzzing.

Larry appeared. She shoved her suitcase closed. He took it and ran out of the room. She pulled on her sandals and followed thankful she really hadn't taken out anything the night before. She grabbed her overnight case.

An armed soldier stood in the living area. He nodded at her. "I'm here to take you to the ship." Dangling on his arm were some masks, which he eased off and handed to them.

"Thank you." Susanna slipped hers over her face, trying to forget how suffocating it felt.

Jeanie glared at it. "Yuck! It's ugly."

"Put it on," Larry directed. "You don't want to breathe in the ash. It will turn to concrete in your lungs and-"

"I get the picture," she huffed back. "What about Leli?" The cat yowled from his carrier.

"I'll take care of it for you, miss." From inside his green field jacket, he pulled out a balled up net like substance. He knelt down talking softly to the cat. Placing the milky ball on the top, it immediately oozed snugly around the carrier. The soldier smiled up at Jeanie. "Your cat will be fine."

"What is that?" Susanna wanted to know. She'd never seen anything like it before.

"Scientist who discovered it just calls it Goo." He got up. "We really need to get moving." He pulled on his own mask and gathered up two suitcases. "You need to come with me." His voice sounded strange through the filter.

Larry took the last suitcase and Susanna shouldered her overnight bag. Jeanie shrugged her backpack on and gathered up the carrier. "Feels kind of warm."

Another quake hit the house and the wood cracked ominously. The three glanced at each other and rushed out. They boarded the same ancient bus which had brought them to the house and got their first look at some of the people they'd be colonizing the new planet with.

Susanna noticed a couple with three young children, an older man with a shaggy beard, and a young man with a Husky. The dog tried to jump forward stopped short by a sharp tug of its leash. There were several scientists she thought looked familiar and a mother with a teen about Jeanie's age.

"Sit here," Larry guided her into a seat. Jeanie sat beside her awkwardly balancing the carrier and her backpack. Their brother stood in the aisle.

With a shake the bus rolled over the ash coated ground. Susanna heard the soldier tell the driver, "One more stop."

"Cutting it close," the uniformed man replied.

"Not our timing."

She turned her eyes to look out the window. The sky overhead had turned an ugly rolling black, though there were colorful pink and gold wisps scattered here and there.

"Creepy," Jeanie observed, her comment accented by a cry

from Leli. "Easy," she tried to soothe the cat." I don't like it either."

The bus lurched to a stop and the soldier got off. Her heart beating fast, Susanna silently urged him to hurry. She had the strongest feeling they didn't have much time. A screech announced the door opening and a young man got on the bus, holding the hand of girl who was maybe two or three.

"Go!" the soldier ordered the driver.

Groaning the bus shuddered forward. The new arrival lost his balance and Larry reached out to steady him. She barely got her arm around little girl in time to keep her from falling. Susanna smiled. "You're okay."

Frightened blue eyes blinked at her before the child backed against her father's legs. He reached down and pulled her into his arms. "It's okay, Krissy. Tell the nice lady thank you."

Blonde curls bobbed as she shook her head, hiding her plump face against his neck. He smiled apologetically. "Sorry. My niece isn't used to strangers."

"I thought she was your daughter." Susanna closed her mouth. That had been a stupid thing to say.

"Understandable," the man said. He took the seat opposite her, his niece sitting on his lap. "My sister," his face shadowed. "Died a few weeks ago."

"I'm sorry," she heard her brother say. "If you need someone to talk to, I am a pastor."

She noticed the varied reactions on the bus, a couple of disgusted looks, a few curious ones, and from the man across from her, relief.

"That's good to know." He offered his right hand, while his left kept hold of Krissy. "Kal Devon."

Her brother took it. "Larry Henry. My sisters Susanna and Jeanie."

"And my cat Leli," Jeanie added, a slightly hurt tone in her voice.

"Kitty?" Krissy slid off her uncle's lap and tried to peer into the carrier.

The cat hissed and the little girl retreated against Kal's legs.

"Don't blame him." He hugged the girl. "Kitty doesn't like traveling," he gently told her.

"Okay." Krissy shyly smiled.

"You seem to be good with children." Susanna shifted. The seat wasn't comfortable and as lumpy as before.

"Lots of practice." Kal didn't elaborate, instead he asked Larry, "I take you're a Christian."

"We all are."

"Glad to hear it." He took a breath. "If this hadn't happened today, I could have introduced you to the others."

"Are there a lot?" Susanna wanted to know.

"Enough." He lowered his voice. "I'd watch Lin Dragoon, if I were you."

"Why? She seems friendly enough." The bus jolted and Larry had to hold tightly to the overhead bar. Susanna hoped he didn't lose his balance.

"Seems, yes." Kal shook his head. "It's nothing I can put into words."

"Warning from the Holy Spirit?" her brother asked. She knew he believed fully in the 'Gifts of the Spirit'.

"Could be. I've also heard rumors about them finding something on Galilahi. What I don't know. I do know they didn't tell the White House."

Jeanie chimed in. "And just why would the President need to know anything?"

"Long story." He managed to get Krissy to sit on the seat. She bounced as the bus did, giggling. "My sister was an aid to him. The night before she died, she made mention of an important discovery. Next day." He glanced at the floor before continuing. "She was killed in a freak hover accident."

Susanna felt like she'd been kicked in the stomach. Hard. She gasped.

"Are you okay?" Larry bent down to check on her.

"Fine." She touched the gentle swell. "I think the baby kicked." She wasn't telling the truth and she could tell from the slight squint of her brother's eyes, he didn't believe her.

"Baby?" Krissy pointed at Susanna's stomach.

"Yes, Krissy," her uncle confirmed, "baby."

Her head cocked to one side as if trying to decide if she believed him or not. The Husky in the back made its famous howling like bark. "Doggy!"

Kal managed to get an arm around her before she ran back to see it. "No, Krissy. Leave the doggy alone."

Her face clouded and Susanna wondered if the child was going to cry. Just as quickly she changed her mind and she climbed over her uncle to see outside. "Ship!"

Chapter 5

Larry gave a low whistle. "Had no idea we could build something like that." He could tell the basic design but not much about the shape. The falling ash obscured most of it.

"Newest design," Kal explained to him. "The *Namid* has all the advances we've managed to learn from all the previous colony ships."

"They're not using the same ship?" That surprised Larry. He'd thought to conserve money they would have made the trip to whatever planet they were colonizing and brought the ship back once emptied.

"No. Each ship is designed to be taken apart once it's landed, so the various parts and compartments can be used to help establish the colony."

"Expensive."

"Practical."

"One way trip," Susanna interjected.

"I hope you understood that." Something in Kal's voice triggered a protective instinct in Larry.

"Of course. I wouldn't be here otherwise." His sister's hand protectively touched her stomach.

"They'll put you in the weightless chamber," Kal told her. "It will protect you and the baby from the G's during takeoff." He reached back and straightened his niece's white T shirt. "Same for Krissy and anyone else they think might not do well during lift off."

"Is it bad?" Jeanie's oval face reflected her worry.

"Not like the first few. Just mildly uncomfortable." He grinned. "In the old days of the space shuttle and launching satellites, they used rockets to break gravity. The *Namid*," he pointed out the window, "though you can't see it clearly, takes off more like a sky hover."

Larry suddenly understood. "You mean it takes off horizontally and eases up into the air."

"Essentially, yes."

Jeanie sighed in obvious relief. "Doesn't sound so bad."

"I've done the test flights. It isn't." He looked sad. "My sister was so proud of me."

"But how did you test it without being spotted?" Susanna wanted to know.

"Was my sister's job. Besides, with so few left in the state, I doubt it was seen by anyone not already on the base."

"I mean—,"

"I know. You start throwing words like classified and national security around, and the curious stop asking questions. If they don't, then the threat of going to prison does."

Susanna nodded. "I understand."

"Bet you do." The bus rattled to a stop.

"They need you on the bridge, sir," the soldier informed Kal.

"Tell them I'll be there as soon as I take Krissy to Dr. Upala."

"Yes, sir."

"You're our pilot?" Larry wanted to know.

"Back up pilot." Kal gathered up his niece making sure her mask and then his were in place. "You might want to come with me, Susanna."

"Go ahead," her brother agreed. "We'll find you later."

"Just go to sick bay."

"Thanks."

"Least I can do for you."

Kal left first running across the ash covered ground. Susanna followed more slowly, tightly clinching her overnight bag. Larry motioned Jeanie to go, grabbing their suitcases. The others rushed out behind them. He found a large hatch open and took a brief moment to admire the pearl like surface of the ship.

"I'll take that for you, sir," a young air man offered though Larry couldn't see his face through the mask. They were in what appeared to be the airlock area. The walls were brown he noticed.

It took Larry a moment to realize the soldier meant their bags. "Thank you." He turned them over while another officer motioned the group up metal stairs.

"Last group," the soldier from the bus reported.

"Good." He recognized General Borromeo's voice. The big man's hand pressed a flat plate on the side and there was a hiss as the door slid closed.

"Leli stays with me," Jeanie objected when a soldier tried to take her cat.

"Easy, Miss." The general removed his mask and offered her a warm smile. Funny, Larry had thought the man rather foreboding when he'd first met him. "All animals are being taken to our vet, Dr. Baker. She'll make sure Leli is safe in a zero G chamber." He lowered his voice. "You don't want your cat to be uncomfortable do you?"

Jeanie bit her lip and shook her head. "Are you sure he'll be okay?"

"You have my word as an officer and a gentleman. Corporal Lewis, would you escort Leli to his launch seat?"

A dark haired young man approached and reached out his hands. "I promise Leli will be safe."

Reluctantly Larry's younger sister handed over the carrier and the growling cat. "I'm gonna want to see Leli as soon as I can."

"I'll take you myself," the corporal promised with a shy smile. He took the carrier and hurried down a long corridor and toward the back of the ship. The man with the Husky sprinted after them.

"Your berths are upstairs," Borromeo said, turning away.

"Thank you." Larry took his sister's arm and the two climbed the narrow rungs. On the next level they were met by a woman wearing a bright smile and a brown jumpsuit. "You must be Lawrence and Jeanie Henry. This way, please." The green passage way seemed a bit narrow. She pressed her hand against a clear panel. "Once we're in space I'll show you how to program this to your handprint. Your quarters are here, Major. Your sisters have the one right next to you." The door slid open. "You'll want to secure the webbing at once. We might not get much warning before we launch."

"Thank you?" He allowed his unasked question to hang.

"Trish O'Malley. If you'll follow me, Miss Henry."

"Jeanie," his sister groused back.

"Jeanie," Trish conceded. "Your bags should already be there in one of the overhead compartments. You will have a bunk mate," she told Larry, "but he's busy at the moment."

He'd wondered if officers would have the same privileges like not sharing a cabin. Evidently, not the case, still he understood the need to conserve space. "Thanks again."

"My pleasure." She took Jeanie next door.

Larry wasn't sure if either bed had been chosen yet, so he just picked one figuring he and the other man could decide later.

There was a twin sized mattress on each side of the room, a closed overhead compartment and a closet he suspected was the head.

Remembering Trish's warning, he picked a bed and pulled the odd webbing, which was like what the solider had put on Leli's carrier, over his body and began the hardest part of their journey. Waiting.

Chapter 6

Susanna followed Kal Devon through a maze of colorful corridors or at least that was how it seemed to her. He finally stopped before a white door emblazed with the familiar red coiled snake emblem of the medical profession. It slid open and he walked into the glaring clean room.

"Amira!" he bellowed.

A figure hurried out from a side room. "You would have made a good general," she teased, a wide smile on her full lips.

"Good thing I never joined the military then." He put his niece down. She clung to his brown pants.

"Hello, Krissy," Dr. Upala greeted, kneeling down so she was on the same eye level as the toddler. "Remember our talk about staying with me while your uncle helped fly the ship."

Blue eyes gazed imploring upward. Susanna wondered how Kal could resist the youngster.

"It's only for a little while," he promised. Kal went to one knee and hugged the child. "As soon as I can I'll come get you and take you to our quarters." Reluctantly he got up. "Take good care of Krissy."

"You know I will." The doctor picked up the little girl. "Go quick. It'll be easier."

He nodded and hurried out.

Krissy started to cry. Amira patted the toddler's back. "If you'll come with me, Dr. Gates. I've been told we might not get a lot of warning." She led Susanna down a narrow hallway and through yet another door. "Zero G chambers," she explained, indicating the odd tubes set in a circular pattern around the room. "Let me get Krissy settled first." Her hand rested on the clear panel and it opened. Two hands reached out. "Take care of her, Joyce." She secured the tube and came over to another one.

"Will Krissy be all right?"

"Joyce is my pediatric nurse. She'll take good care of the girl." The tube opened. "This one is yours."

Crawling inside, Susanna barely remembered in time to grab a hold of the interior metal bars before her body began floating up.

"There's safety netting. Make sure you secure yourself. Wouldn't want you to fall in the event the generators fail."

"That's reassuring," she shot back, doing as instructed. Her stomach lurched slightly and she hoped she wouldn't get sick.

"There's some motion sickness pills in the emergency kit."

"Read my mind. Thanks."

She heard the doctor laugh and the hiss as the door closed. Her fingers opened the kit, found the pill and swallowed it with water she found in a neighboring kit with snacks and other drinks in it. Taking a deep breath she told her pounding heart to calm down. Everything was going to be fine.

"Right, Lord?" she questioned the only person who would be able to hear her. For a moment she would have sworn someone hugged her. It reassured her and she felt her body relaxing. "Thanks," Susanna whispered overwhelmed with how God answered her simple prayer.

A shudder shook her tube. She knew it had nothing to do with any movement of the ship. If what she'd seen outside was any indication, Yellowstone was close to blowing. Having studied the effects the eruption was going to have on the planet, she didn't envy her parents, or anyone else who had to stay behind.

The movie she'd seen made years ago on one of the educational channels had painted a very positive picture of the outcome. From the research she'd done their story was very far from the truth. Once the super volcano actually erupted it would belch tons of ash, rock and gases into the atmosphere. If what happened with Mount St. Helens and others in the past were any blueprint, the material would encircle the globe and block sunlight.

Once the sun was blocked it would have a profound effect on crops, plants and wild life. With no way to grow enough food for the surviving population, millions would die. So would the animals and trees and flowers and just about everything she'd come to hold dear in her life.

"It's so unfair, Father." Tears threatened and she tried to choke them back with no success. Seemed being pregnant gave her permission to give full vent to her feelings since people acted as if it were normal and excusable.

The ship shook again more violently. Hanging there in weightlessness, she didn't actually feel it except for the gentle swinging of her harness. "We're running out of time," she breathed. "Oh, God, please," she put a hand on her stomach. "Please, let us make it out of here."

Chapter 7

The second violent shake alerted Larry to the fact they were running out of time. He knew ash fall was generally a precursor to an eruption, but since no super volcano had gone off in man kind's written history, if the archeologists were to be believed, and most of the volcanologists were only guessing at what warnings they might get beforehand. There was always the possibility it would blow with the ship still on the ground.

"I can't believe you mean for us to die," Larry told God. "You brought us here for a reason, not just my dream of going into space and seeing other planets." He took a deep breath. "Please, be with our parents and help them through what is coming and accepting their loss of us. I know it was hard on them." Understatement, yet given the choice, they'd wanted their children to live.

"And be with our pilots, especially Kal, Father. I know he is going to be special to our lives." Okay, where had that come from he wondered, though he had no doubt God knew. Wasn't the first time he'd prayed for something and hadn't understood the reason for it until later.

"Prepare the new world we're going to for our arrival and give us wisdom on how to establish a colony. And you know, it would be really great if You were more of a center to it than politics and correctness." Maybe a futile prayer. He had no way of knowing.

Another thought came to him so he kept going. "You know, Susanna and I are still young." Of course God knew that. Larry just wanted to say so to organize his mind.

"If there is someone in this group for us to marry, I thank You that You'll make it clear in Your time. Same for Jeanie when she gets older."

Rocking started and he hoped the ship was moving and it wasn't a worse quake. Or Yellowstone blowing.

The door swished open and Kal stuck his head in. "Hey, would you mind coming up to the cockpit and saying a prayer as we lift off?"

Who was he kidding? Larry would love to be there as they launched. "Sure." He undid the harness and trailed after Kal. The corridors changed from green to blue.

"Crew quarters," Kal explained like he'd read Larry's mind. "Agro is orange and right next to the hatch area. Engineering is red." He chuckled. "I think someone was fond a certain old TV series from the nineteen sixties."

"Before my time and my parents."

"Mine, too. Funny how those old classics seem to stick around." He stopped before a door painted navy. "We're here."

"Sure no one else minds I'm here?" Larry felt uneasy.

"The general insisted." They entered a narrow passageway "Security thing," Kal said, "Like they did for the air hovers."

"Yeah. Sure helped solve the hijacker problems." After the events of September 11th back in 2001, there had been a brief period of years with more attempts to use planes as bombs. The airlines had tried numerous solutions and had finally developed a short corridor between the plane and the cockpit. It had two doors making it difficult for hijackers to get through. It also gave the crew time to press the 'Red Button' alerting the ground there was a problem. They could then close the outer door which allowed the pilot to flood the sealed chamber with gas, keeping the hijacker prisoner until the plane could be landed.

Which made Larry stop and think. "They afraid someone on board would try and hijack the ship?"

Kal frowned. "I don't think so. General Borromeo assured me it was just in case of a hull breach."

"I take it there's an auxiliary bridge."

"You betcha."

The last obstacle opened and Larry stepped into the bridge or cockpit as Kal kept calling it. He just stared in wonder. Immediately in front of him was a huge window area, allowing for a great view outside. There were various colored chairs scattered about with people manning stations. In the center a comfortable green chair was mounted and it slowly turned.

"Glad you agreed to come," the general greeted, looking crisp in his khaki uniform and military crew cut.

"He shouldn't be here," Dragoon objected. Her dark eyes glared at him from her place beside the black man. He wondered if what Kal hinted at wasn't correct.

36

"I thought it appropriate to have a prayer said before we left Earth." Borromeo's chocolate eyes narrowed. "I trust it's not a problem."

She huffed and stalked away to a chair, plopping down and crossing her arms. Deliberately she turned her face away from the group.

"She's been up all night," one of the nearby crew explained.

"No excuse for bad manners." The general gave Larry a warm smile. "I'm glad you're aboard. Will be nice to have a preacher."

Completely puzzled by the sudden turnabout since Borromeo, when he'd first met him, hadn't been very friendly, Larry replied. "Thank you, sir."

"Sir," an officer interrupted. "Just got a call from Dr. Byer. He says the quake readings are off the scale and if we're leaving, we'd better go now."

Borromeo nodded. "Understood. Everyone secure your harnesses. Devon, find our guest an empty chair. It's too late to take him back to his quarters."

"Aye, sir." Kal flashed Larry a smile and pointed behind him. "Got an empty one there."

"Thanks." Hurrying over, Larry slipped into the chair and made himself secure. He twisted so he could see out despite the fact his place was near the back of the bridge.

"Begin taxiing." Borromeo sat back seeming completely at ease.

There was a slight jar and the huge ship eased forward. Larry had no idea how they could see with the heavy ash fall. He released a quick prayer asking God for a safe lift off and that they didn't encounter an unexpected crack in the asphalt.

"Byers is screaming," the officer reported again. "I'm guessing Yellowstone is about to blow."

"We'd better hurry then," the general returned. "Take her up, Lieutenant Conners."

"Aye, sir," a voice answered. Larry couldn't see the pilot.

The *Namid* shuddered and picked up speed. He could feel the G's slowly increase as he was gently pushed back in his chair. Just when the ship left the ground he had no idea since all he could see was rolling gray ash. Suddenly they were above it and arcing through clear blue sky.

"Look at that!" someone yelled.

A huge plume of burning gray intruded above the clouds. Within it Larry could see shades of flowing orange, house sized rocks and tons of boiling black ash.

"Bank to port," Borromeo ordered. "We want to evade the eruption."

"Byers is yelling about wanting a closer look."

"Inform him if we don't change course he'll get a closer look than he wants."

"Aye, sir." There were some snickers quickly subdued by a hard stare by the general.

"Receiving an inquiry from Seattle's tower," another officer reported. "They want to know who we are, where we came from and what's happening."

"Tell them to seek shelter immediately," Borromeo returned. "And to call FEMA for evacuation instructions."

"Shall I tell them Yellowstone erupted?"

"Should be obvious, but yes."

"Sir, Dr. Byers is reporting massive earthquakes along several fault lines. Says it looks like the entire West Coast is wobbling."

"God help them." The general swiveled in his chair and faced Larry. "Pastor Henry, this would be a good time for that prayer." He turned to the officer keeping a channel open to Dr. Byers. "Put the prayer on ship wide."

"Now wait just a minute," Dragoon objected.

"The *Namid* is under my command, not yours."

"Channel open, sir," the officer reported.

"Pastor Henry, if you would."

His mind went blank. *'Father, what do I say?'* His mouth opened and words poured out. "Father, bless this ship and all aboard. Be with our loved ones we left behind and guide them through this time of trial and fire. Prepare our new home for our arrival and soften hearts for those who await us." Now that was odd but Larry knew not to question God about it. "Thank you for a smooth flight and without incident, that we are patient and loving with each other, and we remember that You are our provider and protector. Help us to remember our home, Earth and to tell our children and theirs about it. In your son's blessed name, Amen."

"Thank you, Pastor Henry," Borromeo quietly said. "Com

off."

Silence fell over the bridge. Dragoon threw an angry glare at the general, but said nothing. He simply looked at her with the well-known military superiority stare. Yet, something in the exchange told Larry the battle between the two was far from over. He doubted it would bode well for the leadership over the new colony they were trying to establish.

An odd lurch in his stomach told him they'd left Earth's gravity. The view before him was amazing—the blue white orb of their home against the star studded velvet darkness of space. Unwillingly his eyes drifted below to the spreading cloud of death quite visible from their vantage point.

"Dear Father, help the survivors," the general muttered.

Chapter 8

Days later Susanna woke up in her quarters and stretched languidly. Life on board the *Namid* had sort of fallen into a routine. Jeanie uncharacteristically got up early and had her breakfast with a couple of other teen girls she'd found on board and several of the younger Air Force officers. Luckily, her sister had had the good sense to date men in a group setting. Even Lin Dragoon had told the girls they were too young to become serious yet with anyone.

Leli raised his ginger head urping inquisitively at her. He slept with Jeanie but when she left in the morning he climbed down and joined Susanna. His foot rested almost protectively against her growing stomach. Dr. Upala had assured her the ship would arrive on Galilahi long before her baby was due. And with the new Jump Drive or JD as the engineers lovingly called it, she believed the doctor.

"You need to move, Leli. I want to get up." The cat stubbornly put his head back down and refused to move. "Come on now," she teased. "You know Kal, Krissy, and Larry are waiting to have breakfast with me." Leli closed his eyes. Gently she pushed his suddenly heavy body toward the edge of the bunk. "Don't make me dump you on the floor." Opening his eyes he glowered at her and made a great show of rising to his feet, stretching his long form, and looking disdainfully at her. His tail twitched a couple of times before he leaped down.

She laughed at his antics, getting up and going through her morning routine. Putting on a maternity dress she'd bought before leaving, she settled the draping blue fabric dotted with yellow flowers. It made her feel like she was a walking spring garden.

"You behave, Leli," she warned the cat. He didn't give her a response since his head was buried in his dish. Eating was much more important to him than she was. Jeanie always remembered to feed the cat. He'd been her responsibility since he'd moved in with their folks.

Thinking of them made Susanna want to cry and a few tears escaped down her cheek. They would never know their grandchild. Or any of them since she figured both her brother and sister would eventually find someone to marry. She dried her face by wiping it with her hand. There was no mirror so she hoped her eyes wouldn't be red.

Out in the hall she quickly made her way to the common area. The dining hall, the exercise room, the day care with a play room, there were many more children on board than she'd first realized, a game retreat for the teens and those adults who liked to play them as well, and a chapel, were all located there. The walls were painted neutral beige. She guessed someone thought the color restful.

Kal waved at her and Krissy hopped down to run over and hug her legs. Gently she loosened the little girl's arms and took her hand to take her back to her uncle. The toddler climbed back in her chair and stuffed a piece of waffle in her mouth.

"Where's Larry?" she asked as she sat down, after helping herself to a cup of decaf tea.

Kal pushed the bowl of strawberries over to her. "Said something about counseling a couple before they decide to get married and asked if I'd save him a place." He pointed to the empty spot across the table.

Sounded like her brother. Susanna helped herself to some strawberries and grabbed a couple of waffles. She passed on the bacon and sausage. Others began to drift into the room and the noise level slowly rose.

"Ever wonder what we're going to eat on the, our new world?" Kal's pale blue eyes met hers.

"Hadn't really thought about it." She sipped her tea, dropping her gaze to her half empty plate.

"That chair is taken," he told someone trying to take the place he'd saved . "I think we're going to be amazed how God has prepared this planet for us."

"Do they ever talk about the other colonies?"

"Officially no." He leaned toward her while dodging Krissy's oatmeal covered hands. "A rumor I heard is that one colony," he glanced around and lowered his voice. Susanna had to strain to hear him. "They'd encountered intelligent dragons."

"That would certainly undermine the popular thought mankind was the only species made in God's image."

"Tell me about it," he agreed pulling back to greet Larry.

"How'd it go?"

Her brother sagged into his chair. "You don't want to know."

"That good," Susanna returned.

Her brother shook his head and flashed Kal a thankful smile as he poured Larry a cup of coffee. Cream and sugar were already there. Funny, she hadn't thought Kal knew her brother so well.

"Seems the couple only wanted a three year contract marriage and then decide when it ended, if they wanted to stay married." Larry took a swig. "I just came from talking to Dragoon."

Kal glanced curiously at Larry. "What did she say?"

"No contract marriages." He put his mug down.

"Well, that's good isn't it?" Susanna couldn't see why it wouldn't be. "It means she wants stability."

Larry frowned. "I'm not sure what she wants."

"Gave you political double talk, huh?" Kal gave him a knowing smile.

"Yeah. I think I'll talk to the general later." He picked up his mug again. "Why do I get the impression this colony is going to be divided?"

"We can pray it isn't," she reminded her brother.

"Done." Krissy pushed her plate away. "Want more milk."

"Please," Kal corrected her.

"Please," she added.

"Be right back." The child's uncle rose and trotted over to the beverage area.

"She's hiding something," Larry said.

"Am not!" Krissy objected.

"Not you, Sweetheart," Susanna assured the little girl. "Let me wipe your hands, okay?" She grabbed a napkin.

Krissy held up her hands and allowed Susanna to clean them.

"You're going to be a great mother," her brother complimented.

"Thanks."

"Your milk." Larry put the plastic tippy cup on the table. "Thanks, Susanna," he said as he sat back down. "I wasn't looking forward to that."

"You're welcome." His words brought a warm glow to her stomach.

"Seen Jeanie today?" Larry wanted to know.

"No. She left early as usual."

"I've noticed she seems to hang out with Corporal Lewis."

"He works with the vet, but you know that." She glanced at her brother. "If you're concerned, maybe you should talk to her."

"Like she'd listen to me."

"You're not Dad." She gulped at mentioning her father. That was a loss she hadn't really dealt with yet.

Her brother glanced away. "Guess I can be glad I didn't turn out like him."

"I take it they were deemed too old to come." Kal leaned back and relaxed in his chair.

"Yes." Larry picked up his mug again.

"Go play?" Krissy stood up and gazed hopefully at her uncle.

Kal chuckled. "You two gonna stay a bit?" They both nodded. "Come on, kiddo. Let's go sign you in at daycare."

She clapped her hands and raced him across the room managing to dodge groggy people carrying mugs of coffee. Krissy stood by the door and her uncle took her hand. He waved at them and the two left.

"He's a good man," her brother commented, putting some sausage in his mouth.

She knew where he was going. "It's too soon. I'm not looking."

"Might want to." He cut a good sized bite of waffle. "Most everyone else is checking out others who are single."

"Are you?" She knew her look challenged her brother.

He shrugged. "Maybe." They ate in silence for a few minutes. "Planning on starting a Bible study tomorrow."

"That's good."

Kal rejoined them. He placed a glass of orange juice on the table. "What are you plans for the day?"

"Is there really a day in space?" Susanna didn't think so. Granted, the lights were lowered in the hallways to simulate night and turned up to indicate day.

"Can't be that bad." Kal winked at her.

"I think pregnant women just get grouchy," her brother put in. "I'll have to ask Amira about that."

"Amira, huh?" The other man grinned. "I don't know of too many who would dare to call her that."

Larry lifted his mug to his lips. "I'm a pastor. I'm allowed."

"If you were a rabbi maybe."

Susanna suspected Kal was enjoying teasing Larry. She stuck a strawberry in her mouth as she listened.

"I wear many hats."

"Can you see him in a yarmulke?" Kal asked her.

She answered, "If I can see Jesus wearing one, I think I can see my brother doing the same."

"Ouch!" He ducked his head. "Remind me not to ever side against you two." His hand swiped through the air. "I'd never win!"

"Try sparing with Jeanie," Larry said. "She was on the debate team."

"When she wasn't dancing," Susanna reminded him.

"God gave her such a gift." Larry shook his head. "I wonder if she'll get to dance on our new world."

"I wouldn't count anything out." Kal drained his juice. "What did Dragoon say about marriages?"

Larry gave Kal a look Susanna knew well. Whatever the leader of their expedition had said, he wasn't happy about it. "Let you know after I speak with the general."

"Wasn't good was it." Kal leaned forward. "I told you she wasn't to be trusted."

"Her opinion and my trusting her are two different issues."

"Are you sure? She's supposed to lead us."

"Enough, Kal." Larry banged his mug on the table. A few people from a neighboring table glanced up in surprise. "I realize you think Dragoon had something to do with your sister's death, but I haven't seen anything to confirm your suspicions."

"Maybe you haven't been watching."

Susanna decided to intervene. "Stop it you two."

"See, you're upsetting my sister."

"You both are," she corrected Larry.

"Maybe you should listen to your sister."

"Like you have a right to say anything!" Larry got to his feet.

"Stop it!" She knew her voice carried but she didn't care. "Maybe you two Men, should stop and think about what kind of example you're setting." Susanna stomped off, or the best she could do considering her condition, pausing at the door to look back. They were both staring at her shocked. Good. Hopefully, they'd think about how they were acting and apologize to each other.

"Hey, Susanna!" Jeanie bounded up and gave her an awkward hug. "And how's my future niece," she spoke to her sister's stomach.

Susanna laughed. Jeanie always talked to the baby. "I needed that. Thanks."

"Larry being a jerk?"

"Just a man."

Her younger sister giggled. "Kind of hard to remember he is one, huh? I think we tend to only think of him as our brother and a pastor."

"I have to agree."

Jeanie dramatically clutched her hands to her chest. "I don't believe it. We agree!"

"Don't let it go to your head."

"Wouldn't dream of it. Hey," she bounced up and down. "Wanna see a glimpse of our new home?"

"We're not close enough to see it are we?"

"Nah. Jack's gotta friend who was part of the one of the recon missions. He loaned the vids to him."

"Jack?"

"Oh, you know, Corporal Lewis."

"Better not let Larry hear you call him Jack."

"Wanna know how he got his name?" Her face split into a huge grin.

She knew how her sister was about secrets. She couldn't share them fast enough. "Not really, but you're going to tell me anyway."

"Course I am."

"All right, how did he get his name?"

"Remember that show we watched all the time? The one where they went through the gates?"

"You mean the one where they based in Cheyenne Mountain?"

"Yeah. His parents were big time Sci-Fi fans. When he was born, they thought Jack was a great name. They kept telling him he'd travel in space one day."

"And so he is."

"Yeah." She fell silent. "Kind of sad really. His folks will never know."

"Ours don't either. Not really."

"Not the same."

"Okay. What aren't you telling me?"

"His folks were victims at the World Science Fiction Convention when the hotel caught fire."

Susanna had been very young when that had happened. "I didn't know."

"He hasn't really told anyone. Didn't want people feelin' sorry for him."

"Bet he's happy about fulfilling his parent's dream for him."

"He is. Sad, too."

"Like him, don't you?"

Her face turned a bright red. "Yeah. He isn't really that much older than me. Sides," she put her hands on her hips. "All the good ones will get took if I don't make a claim now."

Larry had made a similar statement to her in regards to Kal. "You have plenty of time."

"Not like there's gonna be a lot of choices once we arrive at Galilahi. What we got is what we've got." She gave Susanna a knowing look. "Better make a choice yourself if you don't want to get stuck with a loser."

"I'm not in any hurry."

"What about you baby? You wanna a new daddy don't you?"

"That's not fair."

Jeanie grinned. "Never said I played that way." She waved her fingers and skipped off down the hall.

Susanna shook her head and chuckled. The baby kicked and she touched the spot. "Now you stay out of this," she warned. "I'm not in a hurry to find a new husband."

Although if she'd be truthful with herself she more than just liked Kal. *Don't go there,* she warned herself.

Glancing at the time she hurried off to meet with her scientific team. They had prep work to do before they arrived. Once they landed they'd be too busy to bond and discuss what needed to be done. She'd learned that one with various other groups she'd worked with through the years. All her careful planning needed to pay off.

She hummed a praise song she liked as she went to meet with them and ignored the strong desire to return to the cafeteria and to talk more with Kal.

Chapter 9

It was movie night and feeling like a lead pan sat in his stomach, Larry walked into the infirmary. He glanced around at the various beds and blue clad nurses tending patients. Not seeing who he was looking for he turned to leave.

"Hello, Pastor Larry," Amira greeted from one of the side doors. "Do you need something?"

"Uh," he swallowed and tried again. After growing up with two sisters he should know how to talk to women. "You on duty tonight?'

"Always." She smiled at him. "Part of being a doctor."

"Or a preacher."

"Then you understand." She stood in the door and made no move to leave.

"The movie tonight is one of the old classics. Wondered if you'd like to come." He might as well be blunt since she'd probably say no anyway.

"Which one?"

"Uh," he racked his brain trying to remember what Susanna had said it was. "Something about an angel saving a guy's life and him getting a second chance."

"I know it." She pulled off her white coat. "Give me a sec to hang this up." Amira ducked back in the door she'd appeared from.

"Guess that was a yes," he muttered to himself. Now he was glad he'd changed into a nice shirt and combed his hair.

"Call me if you need me," he heard and turned to see Amira coming toward him. "This film is one of my favorites," she told him, hooking her arm through his. "Great to watch during the holidays."

He noticed how her pants and top accented her womanly curves. Larry started talking to divert his attention onto something else.

"My mom," he swallowed quickly to mask his grief, "and sisters like it, too." He just hoped it was the one he thought it was. "They'd mix up a huge batch of buttered popcorn and drink cups of hot chocolate to watch it on Christmas Eve."

She nodded. "Sounds like a wonderful family tradition."

He wondered about her traditions and how she celebrated Hanukkah. Come to think of it, why would she be familiar with the movie? It didn't seem to fit her beliefs.

"We did a lot of stuff like that growing up," he said.

"But not as adults?"

"Harder to do with Susanna traveling constantly."

"And when she was home?"

"Mom and my sisters kept it up."

They'd reached the common area. The tables had been pushed against the beige walls and the chairs were either lined up or put in intimate groups of about four to six.

"Where would you like to sit?" he asked.

"Your sisters coming?"

"Yeah." He glanced around the room and saw them sitting together on the far side. "They're over there."

"Let's join them."

He didn't really like it, but maybe that would be safer. Amira might think he was just being friendly rather than wanting a date. "Good idea."

They worked their way across the room waving at new friends or sometimes stopping to chat briefly. When they finally reached his sisters, Larry was more than ready to sit down.

"Amira, huh?" Kal teased, grabbing a couple more chairs so they join could the group.

Susanna smiled. "Hi, Larry."

"Hi, sis." He gave her a peck on the cheek.

"And why not?" the doctor shot back. "I like movies."

"Where's Krissy?" Larry asked sitting down.

"At the day care. They're running a children's movie for them."

"Good." Jeanie smiled as Jack Lewis joined them. "Krissy wouldn't like this movie."

"Not sure I'm going to," Jack complained. "I'd rather see the one that started the series. You know, the one my namesake is in."

"They'll run that one in a couple of days," Jeanie told him "Didn't you see the schedule?"

"Haven't had time." He sat down.

"The general's been running drills so any of us pilots can land the ship," Kal said.

"Smart," Larry agreed.

"Want something to drink?" Kal asked Susanna.

"Some water would be nice."

"Be right back."

"What about you, Amira?" Larry waited for her reply.

"I'm fine for now. Thank you for asking."

Lifting his eyes he watched people wander in, find chairs, sometimes rearrange them to suit their group, smiling at each other, talking, it was all very familiar.

"Are you concerned what we'll find once we land?" Amira asked Susanna. The doctor leaned closer to hear his sister's answer. The noise level in the room was rising.

"Yes and no. God knew we'd one day be coming. I'm sure it's prepared for us." Susanna shifted. He figured probably to make herself more comfortable. He couldn't imagine how uncomfortable carrying the baby must be. "I think the unknown, even back on Earth, is scary."

"It's more about how you face your own fear," Larry added.

Amira replied. "I understand that. I had to do that every day growing up."

"I remember you saying where you grew up."

"It was part of my everyday life."

"Don't know if I could have lived that way." Susanna put her hand on her side. "Now you behave and get your foot off my rib."

"Don't listen to her baby," Jeanie chimed in. "You need to be comfy, too."

"Thanks a lot, sis."

"My pleasure. I intend to spoil my future niece."

"You don't have to start now."

"Your water." Kal handed Susanna a glass. She took a drink and looked for a place she could put it. "I'll take that," the pilot offered and placed it carefully under his chair.

"Thanks."

"My pleasure."

The lights flickered indicating the movie was about to start. Everyone quieted. The only thing missing, Larry reflected, was the smell of popcorn.

"Before we run the movie this evening, I have a few announcements." Lin Dragoon stepped to the front of the room, dressed in a long black gown with red dragons flowing over the silk.

"You ever talk to the general about the marriage thing?" Kal asked Larry.

"Yes. Now be quiet."

"In a few days," the oriental woman continued. "We will be close enough to get our first look at our new home. I've convinced our bridge crew and supporting techs to run a feed down here." Her small hand waved at the screen behind her. "We will be running a continuous image until just before we land."

Larry felt excitement growing in him. Finally, he'd get to see the new home God had prepared for them.

"The matter of marriages has come up." A general murmuring rose up and she raised her hand to silence it. "I realize we all have different viewpoints on this. However, after much discussion," her dark eyes seemed to meet his. "It as been decided in the interest of stability both in our new colony and for the children who will be born there, that the return to the traditional monogamous state will be the norm. If any disagree with the policy, please feel free to talk with me after the movie. Now," she stepped to one side, "General Borromeo would like to say a few words."

The black man stepped smartly to the front. He pivoted to face the audience.

"Looks great in a uniform," Jeanie said.

"Hey," Jack objected.

"So do you."

"Good evening. In a few weeks we'll be landing on Galilahi. I hope all of you will take the time to review the landing procedures. Wouldn't want anyone to fall off their bunk."

His comment was met with a few laughs.

"As most of you know, the *Namid* was made so we could disassemble it and have the beginnings of homes for the colony. Our housing techs trained back on Earth and are asking if any of you are interested in helping them, it would be muchly appreciated."

Larry wondered if the use of the word muchly was deliberate or a slip of the tongue.

"Thank you, General." Dragoon took center stage again. "I'm sure everyone will be most helpful in the first days of colonization. Now, if we could run the movie." The two left, the lights dimmed, and the opening overture for the old black and white movie began.

"We should have popcorn," Jeanie griped.

"Shhh," Susanna admonished. "Just enjoy the movie."

"Easy for you to say."

Sneaking a glance at his sister, he saw the tears streaming down Susanna's face. She must really be missing their mother. His own throat tightened and he forced himself not to shed any tears. He felt a hand over his. Glancing over in surprise, he discovered Amira looking at him. She squeezed comfortingly and refocused her eyes on the movie. Thankful for her gesture of kindness, he settled back and enjoyed the film.

When it ended a couple of hours later the lights came up. Larry blinked at the sudden change. He watched as people got up and headed for the doors talking quietly or loudly, depending on their age.

"Knew I always liked that movie," Amira commented as she stretched and stood up.

"Oldie but goodie," Kal agreed. "I've got to go get Krissy. Would you like to come with me, Susanna?"

"Love to." She took his offered hand and Larry wondered at the stab of jealousy he felt. After all, he'd tried to encourage her relationship with Kal.

"They make a nice looking couple," Amira said.

Jack chuckled and Jeanie giggled. They started singing the song from the film mimicking the couple from it. When they finished, they grabbed each other's hand.

"See ya later," his youngest sister called, waving back at him before they melded into the crowd.

"Don't worry about her. Corporal Lewis is a gentleman."

"He'd better be," Larry returned. "Or else he'll have her big brother to deal with."

"You remind me of mine."

"Really? Where is he?" Larry suddenly wished he hadn't asked the question because of her expression.

"He died during a border skirmish."

"I'm sorry."

"Thank you." Her dark eyes met his briefly. "Would you like some tea? I keep some in my office."

"I'm a coffee man."

She laughed. "I think I can arrange that."

They moved forward and joined the throng working its way out of the large room. Once they reached the infirmary, Amira made some hot water and produced a tea bag and canister of instant coffee.

"This okay?"

"Fine."

After the hot drinks were made, she sat down behind her desk, a sort of white plastic construct piled high with computer discs and surprisingly, paper piles. "My backups," she explained motioning with her hand over the mess. "We can't be sure how long our power supplies will last."

"I realize that I'm not privy to all the plans, but I would have thought solar panels would have been planned in." He sat down on the only other chair and pulled it up close so they wouldn't have to talk loudly. They might disturb her patients in the next room.

"They are." She took a sip. "But we have a limited supply and if one gets broken, there won't be any way to replace it."

"Hadn't thought of that." He shook his head. "Guess I kind of assumed our lives would be pretty much like they were at home."

"I doubt our technology will last even through our lifetimes. Probably less once couples and families start their own farms outside the main colony."

"There are things they haven't told us, isn't there?'

"There are things that I haven't been told." She set her mug down. It had a cartoony figure asking 'Is there a doctor in the house?' He wondered where she'd gotten it.

"Like what?"

"Not sure." Tiredly she rubbed her temples. "I've been part of the main planning group since almost the very beginning. When Brad Lane stepped down as the leader and Lin Dragoon took over, there were changes." She blinked. "I know she tried to get the general replaced with one from her own country. The Air Force refused."

"I got the impression," he perched his own cup on a barely open space on the desk. "When I talked with Borromeo, the two of them don't exactly see things the same way."

She nodded. "They put on a front for the rest of us."

"Appear united to keep the group together, but argue back

stage."

"Pretty much." She tapped her nails on her desk. "I shouldn't tell you this," she glanced nervously around. He guessed to make sure they wouldn't be overheard by someone on her staff. "I know the general is trustworthy. I don't know about Dragoon."

"You aren't the first to say that."

She smiled tentatively. "We worked at making this colony as international as possible."

"And I'd bet Dragoon wanted to change more than the general." He could tell from her look his assumption was correct.

"This was the last colony ship going out. Most of the specialists had been decided on at least a decade earlier."

Vaguely he remembered reading articles, normally buried deep in the news, about how some countries refused to relocate their populations farther south. The "Needless American Panic" regarding Yellowstone was considered propaganda until the constant earthquakes started. "Her country realized too late didn't it?"

"They probably lost millions." Amira sighed sadly. "We did manage to get some on the earlier ships and a few on this one. I guess there was all sorts of political infighting and some funding got dropped. I'm not really sure how the *Namid* got finished."

"Maybe Lane stepping down and Dragoon taking over was part of it."

"Maybe." She lifted her mug. "But Lane and his family, he had three children, lost their place on this ship. And Dragoon is single."

"I didn't know." He didn't like the implications.

"I think they were sent south." She shrugged. "I don't really know."

"God does. I'm sure He's looking after the survivors."

"Have you seen the models?" Amira flipped on her computer and pulled up a file. "They aren't very promising. The best survival rate was calculated at five to ten thousand people."

"It's only a guess. I doubt the scientists who came up with those figures are even sure." He tried to smile. "My sister is one and she's always happy when she's proven wrong." Of course, that was after the years of debate and research. He didn't need to tell the pretty doctor. She probably already understood.

"How could God put people through this?"

"Trust me." He dared to reach out and take her hand. "God

isn't through with Earth yet. There's a lot of prophesy needing to come to pass."

"My parents kept telling me that."

"Maybe you should listen."

"There's nothing written about us colonizing other planets."

He laughed. He'd heard the same argument about the Apollo moon landings. "I think God is big enough to have left some mystery to our lives. Otherwise, we'd have nothing to strive for."

"You're a very strange man, Pastor Henry."

"Larry."

"I'm not sure I should call you that."

"It's okay if I give you permission."

"I'll see." She rose gently disentangling her hand from his. "I have some reports to finish tonight. I've enjoyed our talk."

"Me, too." He sounded lame but it was the truth. "Join me for dinner tomorrow?"

Her dark eyes registered surprise. "If I'm free."

"Great." He got up and handed her his mug. "Thanks for the coffee."

Chapter 10

Susanna was still up when Jeanie came in. Leli urped and hopped off her lap to rub against her sister's ankles. "Have fun?"

"Figured you'd be asleep," Jeanie mumbled.

"My baby is restless tonight. Keeps kicking me in the ribs."

"Naughty baby," her sister scolded. "You need to let your momma rest."

"That's a first. Normally you take my baby's side."

With a shrug the young woman kicked off her shoes. "What do you think of Jack?" She plopped down the end of Susanna's bed. Leli jumped up and joined her. Absently her sister stroked the tabby.

"I think the better question is what do you think of him?"

"You sound like mom."

"Learned from the best." She felt a pang and shoved it away. Jeanie needed her now. She could mourn her mother later. "Well?"

"I really like him." She pulled her jean clad legs up against her chest and wrapped her arms around them. The cat rested his head on her foot. "He's smart. Makes me laugh. Knows how to have fun."

"But?"

"He isn't a Christian."

"Are any of the young men your age?"

Jeanie shook her head. "I don't feel like I should be nun."

"Wrong religion."

"You know what I mean."

"I do." She shifted trying to get more comfortable. Leli lifted his head and blinked at her before stretching one of his front paws and resettling. "Have you asked God about it?"

"Now you sound like Larry."

"History is filled with men and women who won their future spouse to the Lord."

"I know." She lowered her chin to her knees. "You think I'm going to marry him?"

"You might."

"And it's not like I have a lot of choices, huh?"

"I think you should ask God about what His choice is for you and patiently wait for your future husband."

"Easy for you to say," Jeanie grumped. She lifted her head and her nutmeg eyes took on an impish gleam Susanna knew well. "Have you done that?"

She winced. "Ouch."

"You haven't!" Her sister clapped her hands gleefully.

"I honestly hadn't thought about remarrying."

"I think Kal likes you."

"And I like him."

"Just not 'that' way."

"It's too soon." Her eyes welled and she wiped at them.

"I didn't mean to make you cry!" Jeanie sounded distressed.

"It's," she took a breath and tried again. "It's just part of mourning process. Plus," she put her hand on her swollen stomach. "My hormones are running amuck."

"If I had a credit for every time I've heard that," Jeanie joked.

"Doesn't make it any less true."

"Yeah, I know." Jeanie stroked Leli. He made a faint noise and filled the room with his loud purr.

Susanna and her sister looked at each other both coming to the same realization.

"We haven't talked like this for a long time, huh?" Jeanie straightened her legs and put her back against the wall. Leli resettled himself on her leg.

"No. Feels good."

"Yeah."

"Guess I've been busy with my work."

"It's not like you lived with mom and dad."

"Gary," she choked slightly. "And I did plan to visit."

"Not your fault you were the world's little scientific darling."

"The way you say that makes it sound like something awful."

"I asked mom once why you had to be gone all the time." Jeanie pulled Leli onto her lap and scratched under his chin. His eyes half closed in pleasure. "She told me it was because God gave and made you a special gift."

Susanna started. She'd never thought of herself in those terms. "Leave it to mom."

"They're really proud of you, ya know. Larry, too."

"Not you?"

Jeanie grinned. "I wasn't happy at first when I got to high school. My teachers were always comparing me to you. But mom she told them to stop and that I was a different kind of blessing with special gifts." Her sister took a deep breath. "They stopped."

"Doesn't mean you aren't smart."

Her sister giggled. "Oh, I'm smart. I got a look at my IQ. It's high like you and Larry."

Susanna moved so she could put her hand on Jeanie's arm. "God gifted you in the arts. You should be proud of that."

"I am." She bit her lip like she was trying to make a decision. "There was a scout talking to me from one of those fancy dance schools. Told me he could arrange a scholarship if I wanted it." Her eyes drifted down. "I was thinking about it."

"I'm sorry. This must all seem unfair to you."

Jeanie shrugged. "Wouldn't have mattered anyway, not after Yellowstone blew."

What was it Larry always told her? "I know this is going to sound cliché but when God closes one door,"

"He always opens another. I know. I could still be on Earth and maybe not survive at all. Do you know if," Jeanie paused like she was considering her next words. "If any of the colonies failed?"

"I honestly don't know."

"I wonder if there is a way to find out."

"Now don't you go and get yourself in trouble."

With an innocent look that said 'who me?' Jeanie replied, "They probably purged all the info from the computer anyway. Gov never has been big about admitting to their failures."

Later when her sister was sound asleep, Susanna considered her sister's words. Had any of the colonies failed? According to her team none of the new worlds kept in contact with Earth or even each other. If the flight path she'd seen was correct, they had and would be passing several. Did she dare do what she was thinking? And would any on her team think it good idea or report her to Ms. Dragoon, whom she had little doubt would prevent any such attempt.

"Only one way to find out," she said out loud.

From the bunk above Leli answered as if she'd been talking to him. She laughed. "Go back to sleep you silly cat."

Morning brought the usual routine and passed quickly. Late in the 'afternoon' she paused in her work. Susanna had not forgotten her sister's question. Since the outside room was so quiet she knew her staff had left for the day. Most of their work wouldn't really begin until after they landed. What they spent their time doing was rechecking equipment and making plans to explore their new home.

Her eyes drifted to the Com unit sitting against the tan wall. It was similar to the old manual ones used so many centuries ago she couldn't recall it from the history she'd studied. Some resourceful soldier had found it and suggested it should go along. The general had agreed and there it was

"Do I dare, Lord?" she prayed. Susanna could always use the pretext they needed to test it before reaching the colony. And that brought another question, should she do it herself or involve someone on her team?

"Hungry?"

She jumped and let out a breathless laugh. "You startled me, Kal."

"Sorry." He gave her an impish grin and she took a moment to study his face. Kal was good looking. Maybe not in the holo star way as was popular, but he could hold his own in an even competition.

"Didn't realize how late it was," she answered wondering why her cheeks were burning.

If Kal had noticed her reaction he didn't say so. He grabbed one of plastic white chairs and pulled it up to her construct desk. His finger tapped her computer. "You need to turn that off and come get somethin' to eat." He grinned. "I hear they're playing Jack's favorite movie tonight."

"Again?"

Kal shrugged. "They only brought so many."

"And I'll bet we'll miss them once we don't have power anymore."

He reached across and captured her hand. "Not if you scientific folks come up with a new power source."

His comment caused her to frown. "Do you have any idea why we can't get full access to the survey file?" She'd only discovered that disturbing fact today. Pulling her hand free she opened the file where all the data she needed should be. "For some reason the geological and biological files have been sealed."

"That's strange." Kal came to stare over her shoulder.

"It is. My team is going to need the information, particularly if we want to find a renewal power source."

"Have you asked Dragoon?" His tone sounded doubtful. She knew what he thought of their leader.

"Not yet." She hesitated before she added. "Jeanie asked me an interesting question last night. She wanted to know if any of the colonies had failed." She turned slightly. "Do you know?"

He made a face and reached past her. His fingers deftly played over the keys. Hitting enter he stepped back. A list sprang up on the screen and she scanned it.

"How did you...?" she let her question hang.

"I used my sister's password." He took a deep breath. "Guess they figured no one else knew it so it wasn't deleted."

"How high was her security clearance?"

"Pretty high."

"She must have trusted you a lot." Susanna regretted the words once she said them. "I'm sorry. That was a tactless thing to say."

"I was her added security." He went back and sat in his chair. "I think she wanted someone else to have access. Just in case."

His comment brought even more unpleasant questions to her mind. Had his sister known she was in danger? And if so, why and from whom?

"The list say anything interesting?" he asked.

"Mostly planet names and coordinates. Huh."

"Something?" He sat up straighter, gazing intently at her.

"Survivability stats." She clicked on one. "Murani Prime." Her eyes scanned through the planet density, weather information, and other scientific data. "Probable survival rate less than twenty percent. Threat to human population both from periodic meteor bombardment and large reptilian carnivores. Only possible colonization area a mountainous island surrounded by water on all sides. Number of colonists sent, one thousand sixty three." She saw the size of the island. "Kal, where they sent them wouldn't support the population for more than a generation, maybe two."

"Any contact?" He came back around and bent down to see the screen.

"None." She selected another planet. "Talo Four. Soil lacks

the necessary nutrients to support crops and livestock. Possible danger from large dragon like creatures living in the high mountains." She skipped over the usual data collected. "Small religious sect consisting of five hundred forty two souls settled on T4 with minimum supplies. Possibility of surviving without contact, and trade, less than ten percent."

"Dear, God," Kal breathed. "Are they all like this?"

Fear for her unborn baby, Larry, Jeanie, herself and every colonist aboard filled her. "Let's find out."

Chapter 11

Larry had volunteered to work in the kitchen and help prepare breakfast. Stretching his long legs he stumbled out of bed hoping he didn't wake his bunk mate, if the young man was there. Normally the engineer spent most of his time, and, from what he'd garnered from the brief talk they'd had, the officer slept there as well.

Reminds me of another couple of characters from an old TV show.

A quick check revealed the engineer wasn't there so Larry turned on the lights, cleaned up, got dressed and jauntily headed for the cafeteria. Maybe he'd make waffles. They hadn't had them for several weeks.

As Larry entered the kitchen he grabbed one of the staff. "How come we never have waffles anymore?"

"No one's got the patience for 'em."

After he'd heard that, he mixed up the batter and put one of the privates on the duty cooking the waffles. Others he had busy frying bacon, sausage, and eggs, while he sliced fruits and arranged them on plates.

"Hey, Larry!" Jeanie ran up to him. She took a deep breath and told him, "Susanna didn't come to bed last night."

"Maybe she stayed at her lab. You know she does that sometimes." He gave his youngest sister a smile. "We'll be landing in a few days. I'll bet she's got lots to do."

"Thought of that." She kicked at the gray metal floor. "But she's been careful 'cuz of the baby."

"I'm sure there's no reason to worry, Jeanie." He frowned as his mind drifted back to dinner. Susanna hadn't joined them. And come to think of it, neither had Kal. "Been to your sister's lab?"

"Nah. Just didn't seem like her is all."

"I don't have time to go check" He pushed the plate he was working on aside and started the next. "Why don't you go see if she's still there and let me know."

"I'm meeting Jack."

"Jack will understand."

"But, Larry,"

"Go," he firmly ordered. "Now you've got me worried, too."

"Whatever." She stomped off.

Larry was pretty sure everything was all right, but once Jeanie found their sister and let him know, he'd relax. *I know everything is okay, Lord. Please, direct me as I prepare food for everyone.* A part of him was very excited. He enjoyed cooking as much as being a pastor. This was the first time he was going to be able to use his second passion to bless others. He just hoped he could continue to cook after they landed. The new colony would need good, filling and nutritious food to complete all the work and building they'd need to do in order to survive.

"First batch is ready," the private cooking the waffles reported.

"Get them to the buffet," Larry ordered. "We've already got people waiting."

"Yes, sir!"

The screen was down Larry noticed as he put the fruit plates on the buffet. The first images of their new home filled it. Cocking his head he decided it wasn't very impressive. It was just a twinkling star against a black filled background.

"I'm under whelmed," Jack commented from a nearby table. "Trees. Why are there always trees?"

Larry grinned at the comment since he knew the reference. "I don't see any trees. Besides, it'll be different the closer we get."

"If you say so." Jack glanced around the room. "Where's Jeanie?"

"Sent her to find her sister."

"From what I hear," Jack stared down at his empty coffee mug. "She and Kal were holed up in the lab all night."

Larry had expected her to be working with her team. Kal being there brought a number of questions to mind and some hopes as well. He said, "Maybe she's helping him pick out the best landing spot."

"Yeah, maybe." The younger man hesitated. "Doesn't explain why Ms. Dragoon was so upset about it."

One of the kitchen staff was waving him over. There must be a problem. "I'm sure it's nothing, Jack. Maybe they've just found something unexpected."

"Like in most Sci-Fi stories that's when the trouble begins."

Shaking his head Larry hurried into the kitchen and spent the rest of the morning getting breakfast for everyone. Once the meal was over the lunch crew came on and the breakfast group cleaned up. It was nearly mid-afternoon before he finished. He grabbed a cup of coffee and sat down dumping sugar and cream into it.

"Hey," Jeanie plopped down in the chair next to him.

He remembered she was supposed to let him know about Susanna and it had been hours ago he'd sent her to find their sister. "Well?"

His younger sister frowned. "When I got there, I heard Dragoon lecturing Susanna and Kal about the evils of looking into things they didn't need to know about."

"And?" he prompted when she didn't continue.

"And," she drew a picture with her finger on the table top. "The general intervened telling Dragoon no real harm had come of it and it was only natural they'd be curious."

Larry sipped his coffee and made a face. He'd added too much sugar.

"Susanna said they had a right to know and did those poor people know what they were walking into? Dragoon replied it had been decades ago and it hardly mattered now. Our sister disagreed and demanded to be shown the data that had been kept from them. Fearless leader said no and ended the discussion. She stomped out and gave me a glare like I had no right to be there."

"Is Susanna okay?"

"Yeah. She, Kal and the general got into it so I left to meet Jack and thanks for telling him where I was." She smiled. "He waited for me."

"Point in his favor." Larry was getting to like the young man.

"I really like him."

"Just be careful so I don't have to go all 'big brother' on him."

Jeanie rolled her eyes. "Bet you would have scared Gary off if you'd gotten the chance."

"Doubt it." The family had only met the young man once before the two had gotten married. Larry had been impressed that Gary had been open and honest about his intentions toward Susanna.

"He was a good guy." Jeanie got up and spared a glance at the screen. "Sort of feel like the space family that kept getting lost."

"We aren't lost, Jeanie."

"No, but many are." She leaned over and kissed his cheek. "We aren't here by accident you know."

Her observation surprised him. Larry had no idea Jeanie could think on such deep levels. "So you're not mad at us anymore for dragging you away?"

"Didn't say that." Her face held a sad look. Jeanie was probably missing their parents. "I have to admit though," she touched a finger to her lips. "All these good looking military boys are great compensation."

"Thought you only had eyes for a special one." He grinned at her.

"I ain't blind." She skipped away reminding him of the little girl she'd once been, playing hopscotch and jumping rope out in front of his parents' house with her friends.

"Help her choose wisely, Father," he breathed. Larry took a sip of his coffee and grimaced. He needed to dilute it. Getting up he went to the table where they'd finally set up twenty-four seven dispensers. The closer they got to their new home the more people tended to work all sorts of hours. Evidently that now included his sister. Although what she and Kal had been snooping in concerned him.

Nearby there was another table set up with sandwiches, fruit and other types of food. He grabbed several items and sat back down. His stomach reminded him he hadn't eaten breakfast.

"From the look of your plate, son," General Borromeo sat down across from him. "You'd think we didn't feed people."

"Skipped breakfast."

"It was excellent." The general sipped from a mug. It had a circle with familiar symbols Larry recognized. "Gag gift," he explained. The pastor assumed the black man noticed his interest. "Liked the show myself. Made me think the human race could do anything."

"Before or after you got saved?" Larry started not exactly sure where his question had come from.

"Both." Borromeo smiled. "God tells us things sometimes when we least expect it." He lowered his voice. "Your sister and Mr. Devon found out some things they weren't supposed to know."

"Are they in big trouble?" He was afraid for Susanna.

"Some. I managed to convince Ms. Dragoon I'd handle it and

she didn't need to worry about their discoveries becoming public."

"Don't suppose you'd?" he left the question open.

"I know your younger sister overheard part of it and I'm assuming she told you?"

"Only what happened, not what they'd found."

"You three seem to be very close."

"We are."

"I thought so." He sipped from his mug. "Well, at least Jeanie didn't hear too much. Otherwise, I would have been pressured to confine her for the rest of the voyage."

"That doesn't sound good."

The general sighed. "In the early part of our colonization push, we made some mistakes. We learned from them and corrected the future ones."

"Why all the secrecy?"

Casting his dark eyes around them, the general checked the area before answering. "Some of the first ships were experimental and were manned by prisoners, most of which were volunteers." He shrugged. "I know it sounds inhumane, but many were faced with life imprisonment or the death sentence." He paused. "According to the records there were a few ships that crashed, blew up or vanished. Every failure or success were learned from and fueled the drive to keep pushing outward, making it possible for us to send valued citizens."

"What happened to the successful prison ships?" Larry asked.

"Their ships were on auto pilot with clear destinations." The general's eyes held Larry's. "They were the ones sent to less desirable planets."

"We didn't learn from history." He took a sip of his coffee and made a face. It was cold. "Wasn't that what England used Australia for?"

The general chuckled. "I have to agree, son. I only learned about this five years ago when I was tapped for this mission."

"This is what my sister and Kal learned?"

"Not exactly. I had to explain the entire story to them so they understood what they were looking at." He stretched his shoulders. "Some of the early prisoners received permission to take their families with them."

"Ouch."

"I know. Most however, thought it would be better than staying here."

"Any idea how many actually survived?"

Borromeo carefully set his mug on the table. "Now that's the funny part. Every ship had a special beacon sending a signal back to Earth notifying those in command the vessel had arrived. After that, the colonies were never heard from again."

"I'm surprised the next mission didn't try to contact them as they passed by."

"Who said some of them didn't?"

"That information ever make it back to Earth?"

"I'm really not at liberty,"

"Come on, General. Dragoon wouldn't be so upset and you wouldn't have stepped in if some hadn't."

"There are rumors."

"There's rumor, and there's fact. Which is it, sir?"

"A little of both." He picked up his mug again. "Sorry I can't be more specific."

"How about sharing what you know," Larry suggested with a slight smile touching his lips. "I am a pastor after all and what you'd tell me would be considered privileged information."

"If I were coming to you for counseling, I might agree."

"Can't blame me for trying."

The big man released a deep bellowing laugh. Several in the room cast questioning looks in their direction. "I like you Pastor Henry." He extended his hand over the table. "You can call me Malcolm."

"And you can call me Larry." He took the offered hand noting with approval the man's shake was firm. Borromeo was someone they could trust.

The two spent the next couple of hours talking. Finally, when Larry noticed Susanna hadn't come in to eat he decided he'd better take her some food.

"Thanks for sharing what you know," Larry told Malcolm. "So what happens now?"

Pointing toward the screen where the system of their future home was growing larger the general replied, "We get ready to land."

Chapter 12

General Borromeo had given her access to the information she needed and Susanna intended to take full advantage of it. She opened the file and began studying the data. Her staff had been straggling in and out all day. She'd have to decide who needed to know what. They had a lot of work to do before they landed.

For a brief second she missed Kal's steadying presence. He'd gone off to get some rest and to check on Krissy. The poor little girl had been left at the daycare after the discovery they'd made. She suspected he'd try to make it up to his niece.

"Hmmm, now, let's see what I can find." She tapped a few keys and the information unfurled and revealed itself to her.

Galilahi had a range of volcanoes on the third continent. Byers would want to know that. Most of it looked like massive land building had gone on for centuries. Sort of like Hawaii only on a much larger scale. It wouldn't be habitable and she'd have to have the geologist do a check to see if the ash in the air would affect their colony.

The fact the planet was only twenty-five percent water she already knew since Dragoon had already supplied the information. Dr. Stu Anderson, head of the oceanography team, couldn't wait to explore the new ocean. The information on the aquatic life was sketchy and she figured he'd happily spend the rest of his life discovering the water mysteries of their new home.

Chuck Davis, their combination agricultural and husbandry expert, would need the results of the soil samples, analysis of the grasses, plants and trees, and the average rainfall numbers. This would help him determine what would be safe for the animals to eat. Not to mention they'd need to irrigate the crops. She'd also include what data she had on potential predators.

"I'd better send that to the vet and Dr. Upala as well," she said out loud to herself. In the event an animal or person got injured at least they'd have a base to start with for treatment.

There did seem to be some sort of large carnivorous feline, not to mention a reptile very close to a snake. Susanna shivered. She wasn't afraid of snakes as many others were, but she could truthfully say she didn't particularly like them.

"Hey," Larry stuck his head in the door. Her nose detected an appetizing smell and her stomach growled. "Figured you'd hadn't eaten."

"Thanks. I've been so busy I forgot."

"Can't have you starving my future niece," he teased back. He cleared a spot on her desk and set the plate down.

Ordinarily his remark would have been funny. Because of the information she'd been looking at, the reality of their situation sank in. "Hopefully that won't happen."

"Sorry, sis, I didn't mean to upset you." Larry pulled up a chair.

She picked up the fork and speared some lettuce. "It's just all the data I've been looking over."

"Talked with the general. I understand."

"He seems to be a strong ally."

"Borromeo is, Susanna. He's a Christian."

She looked at her brother surprised. "I didn't know."

"Me either until a couple of hours ago." Larry glanced around. "Where's Kal?"

"Either sleeping or spending time with Krissy."

"You two are going to have your hands full raising two young children."

"Don't you think you're getting ahead of yourself?" She chewed her salad, swallowed, and started the next bite.

"Am I? I think he'd make a good husband for you."

"What about you and Amira?" she shot back.

"Let's see," he counted off his fingers. "First, there's the faith issue. Second, I doubt she actually sees me in a romantic light, third—"

"Are you sure? You two seem to sit together and hold hands during movie nights."

He sat back and stared at her speculatively. "Maybe I'm not ready to settle down."

"Perhaps I'm not either." She took the apple off her plate and set it aside. She'd eat it later.

"Want to know what the male/female ratio is on this ship?" Her brother leaned forward. "About sixty-forty."

"More men or more women?"

"Women. Dragoon wanted to have group marriages."

"But that isn't what she said."

"I know. The more conservative element aboard voiced their opinion." He got up and paced. "Most of us are in our late twenties or early thirties. There are a few over forty, mostly specialists. A small percentage is in their late teens or early twenties. I think there's maybe about fifteen children."

Her curiosity got the better of her. "How many total?"

"Since this was the last ship out, they evacuated as many as possible." Larry stopped pacing and sat back down. "One thousand, four hundred twelve."

He took a deep breath. "From what the general told me, they included a lot of the military still on the base, who weren't originally supposed to part of the mission. He saw no reason to leave them behind."

"Fortunate for them." Her mind absorbed what she'd just been told. "I wouldn't have wanted to suffocate in ash."

"Not to mention having to live with the knowledge."

"There is that." Susanna didn't know if she could have lived with herself if she'd known there were others left behind to die. Not when they could have been saved.

"Done?" He pointed at her plate.

"Yes, thanks." She handed it to him.

Larry got up. "Been to bed yet?"

"No."

"You need your rest, sis." He took on the stern big brother look. "I suggest you turn off your computer and go get some sleep."

She laughed. He used to do that while she was in high school. Often she'd stay up all night and go the entire day before she'd stop if she thought she could get more work done.

"We have several days before we arrive. There's plenty of time," he told her.

"But the sooner,"

"It'll keep." He came around behind her. "Now, either you turn that off or I'm going to do it for you."

She knew he would. "Fine." Quickly she moved the data into another file so she could find it again. She closed out the program and got up. Larry backed up out of her way.

"Bed," Larry ordered.

"Yes, sir!" Susanna gave him a mock salute before slowly

trudging off to her quarters. Glancing down, she couldn't even see her toes. When had her stomach become so large?

Leli greeted her with an urp and stretched over his spot on the bed. He blinked his yellow eyes at her before he closed them again.

"You're going to need to move so I can lie down," she told the cat. Carefully she adjusted herself on the covers, forcing Leli to move. "Told you," she said when he glared at her.

With her head resting on the pillow, her eyes stared at the bunk overhead. Susanna knew she should sleep. Her mind whirled with all the discoveries they'd made about past colonies and the concealed data about their new home.

"Should I try to contact any of them, Lord?" she asked aloud. "Realistically, most have probably lost their technology and not be able to answer, still," the idea persisted. Would it be worth the risk? Or would Dragoon—would their leader what? She didn't have the courage to finish the thought.

A paw touched her arm. Leli started to purr, his claws lightly touching her skin.

"Better keep those sheaved," she warned the feline.

He lifted his leg almost as if he understood her. The cat made what sounded like an inquisitive sound to her and sat down, his tail tucked over his feet.

"You can nap with me." She smiled fondly and scratched along the side of his face. Leli's eyes half closed. "I know you like that."

After a few minutes, he circled a couple of times and settled down in the crook of her arm. Susanna wiggled a couple times trying to get more comfortable. Her eyelids drooped and she promised herself she was only going to rest. There was simply too much to do!

Her next conscious thought was who was shaking the bed and why? Groggily she opened her eyes. The light was on and a shadow hovered over her.

"Hey, wake up or you'll miss dinner."

The owner of the voice registered. "Go away, Jeanie. I just went to bed."

"Aren't you hungry? You're always hungry."

Slowly Susanna sat up. She rubbed at her eyes and shook her head to try and clear it. "What time is it?"

"Ship time?" Susanna nodded. "Around eight."

She'd been asleep for probably five or six hours.

"I'll feed Leli," Jeanie offered. "Come on. Supper."

Leli got up as if he had all the time he wanted. He arched his back and paused to wash a paw.

"They're great pretenders," her sister commented. "Come on, Leli. I want to get *my* dinner."

Susanna smiled as the cat jumped off the bed and followed Jeanie to where his dish was. Her younger sibling retrieved his food, filled the dish and while he was eating, cleaned and filled his water bowl.

Swinging her feet slowly off the bed, Susanna moved her shoulders attempting to lose the stiffness that had set in.

"Not used to overnighters anymore, are ya?"

"Been awhile," she agreed.

"Larry's cooking tonight, so I'm betting it's gonna be good."

"Since when are you a fan of military food?"

Jeanie shrugged. "Larry didn't cook a lot at home, but some of the guys I hang around with are from the mountain. They told me they liked his cooking best."

"And you're going to take their word for it?"

"Yep." She crossed her arms. "You gonna hurry or what?"

"Give me a minute." Her bladder urgently needed to be emptied, one of the disadvantages to being pregnant. She hurried into the bathroom. She almost didn't make it. Susanna was just grateful she and her sister had been given one of the few quarters with its own restroom. Most had to share the public one. If she'd had to go down the hall, she would probably have had an accident.

When she finished she washed her hands and she wished she could check her appearance. Not that Kal seemed to mind how she looked. "Now stop that," she told herself. "You're not looking remember?"

"Talking to me?" Jeanie called.

"Just talking to myself." She came out.

"Bad habit. Could get yourself in trouble."

"I thought it was sign of brilliance."

"Think it only works for holo characters."

Susanna snapped her fingers. "Too bad."

The sisters shared a laugh.

"Didn't you say something about dinner?" Suddenly she was

hungry.

"Good for you, baby." Jeanie lightly tapped her sister's stomach. "Momma needed reminding."

"You're having a bad influence."

Jeanie gave her a cheeky grin. "That's what aunties are for."

Shaking her head, Susanna followed her sibling out and to the cafeteria. A few from her team were there. They waved when they saw her but kept talking. She understood it was the way of scientists. There was just so much to theorize about and they didn't want to stop their discussion.

She took her place in line and filled her plate with all sorts of old favorites. There was a heap of mashed potatoes with gravy, a type of green bean dish dripping in butter and bacon, a nice roast, and several other wonderful choices. Larry saw her as she went through and gave her a smile. His eyes drifted to her plate with a meaningful look.

"Eating for two," she mouthed back.

"Good excuse," he answered the same way.

At the end she decided to come back for dessert and located a place to sit. Jeanie joined her, as did Jack. Susanna glanced around curious as to where Kal was.

"Eating with Krissy tonight in their quarters," Jack informed her as if he'd read her mind. "Think she has a cold and they're afraid she'll cause an epidemic."

"We do live in close quarters. I don't blame Dr. Upala for being cautious." She'd have to find out later how the little girl was. Susanna took a bite of potatoes and enjoyed the taste. "This is good."

"Larry was always the favorite cook." Jack shoveled meat smoothed with gravy into his mouth.

"Ugh. You need to learn some manners," Jeanie told him.

"Hey, I'm a growing boy." His comment almost seemed to have a double meaning. Jeanie glanced away, her face red.

"I won't have that kind of talk in front of my baby. Or my sister." Susanna's tone held a warning note.

Jack played with his food for a moment. "Yes, Ma'am."

"We'll be landing soon." Jeanie seemed desperate to change the subject.

Susanna grimaced. "Guess that means I'll be back in Zero G."

"Safest place for you," Amira said as she sat with them. "Okay, if I sit here?"

"Of course." She was beginning to feel like the doctor was part of their little group.

"A lot closer." Jack pointed to the growing image on the screen.

Jeanie frowned. "Sort of foreboding."

Taking a long look at the planet, she had to agree with her sister. Dark clouds raced across the surface. There wasn't much blue, like the pictures she'd seen of Earth. "Wonder if it's raining."

"Least that would be like home." Jack shoved in another bite of meat.

"You really need to learn manners," Jeanie teased.

What looked like lightening split the clouds. For a brief moment, Susanna thought she saw the image of a huge cat-like head.

Chapter 13

Larry stayed late helping the dinner staff to clean up. He wasn't afraid of honest work and it gave him time to talk with some of them. One of the Airmen took to him immediately, telling him about home and his parents. He learned a couple of the young men had managed to get permission to bring their girlfriends.

"Susie wasn't happy about it," a young ensign, Rob, told him. "Didn't want to be out here safe while her parents," he stopped like he'd just realized something. "Guess my folks are gone, too."

"You don't know that," Larry tried to reassure the other.

"They lived in Casper. It was part of the blast zone. They refused to leave when the government told everyone to evacuate last year."

"They believe in God?"

Rob shrugged. "They went to church."

Larry said a quick prayer for the young man's parents and for Rob. "Planning on marrying Susie?"

"If she agrees. Need to go, Pastor." Rob shuffled off.

He kept working, but heard similar stories from others. Late into the 'night' the kitchen and dining area where finally clean. Larry grabbed a cup of coffee and sat down where he had a good view of their soon to be new home.

"You're up late, Larry." Amira grabbed the chair next to him.

"So are you."

"I'm never off duty."

He understood what she meant. As a pastor he was always on call. "Guess it will be worse once we land."

"Maybe, maybe not." She sighed. "It will be good to see sky again."

"Have to agree there." He was pretty sick of the painted walls and cramped quarters. The area they were currently in was the largest on the ship.

"Sad part is," the doctor shifted uncomfortably. "Is that I already have women asking if I brought birth control along."

"Thought they understood we're here to start a colony."

"They do. But they haven't forgotten about their rights."

Larry knew what she was talking about. Under the first and last woman president, Justine Stoddard, she'd pushed through a bill guaranteeing women certain rights. Quite a feat considering the still male dominated congress. "I'm assuming not all women aboard are from the states." He pretty much knew what the count was, just not where everyone was from.

"Large majority." She stood up and stretched. "I don't believe in a couple of them."

He knew which ones she was probably talking about. "Know what you mean."

"I had a feeling you'd understand." Amira leaned down, giving him a peck on the cheek. "Night."

"Good night." Taking a sip of his now cold coffee, he watched her leave. Amira Upala was one beautiful woman.

"She'll make someone a wonderful wife."

He glanced up as the general took the doctor's vacated chair. "You're up late, Malcolm."

"Closer we get," he motioned to the screen. "The less I sleep."

"Something we need to be concerned about?" He hadn't forgotten his sister's problems with getting some of the information her team needed or the reaction of Dragoon.

"What wasn't said." The general shook his head. "Sorry, son, but I've been in the military too long and have developed an instinct about these things."

"The reports don't tell us everything." He understood what the other man was saying.

"No. I know the missions were hurried for the last few planets. Our time was running out."

"When did the mission before ours launch?"

"About two years ago. The one before that, three, and one before that, ten and before that, fifteen." Borromeo got up. "More coffee?"

"Thanks." He handed his cup to the black man. When the general sat back down, he handed the mug to Larry.

"Only time the missions were launched sooner was at the beginning. When we began pushing out here." He paused to take a sip. "Afterward, they slowed down for a few years, so they could make sure the ships were safe."

"Seems to me," Larry hesitated before he continued. "Once the technology was ready, they should have launched more ships."

"That was the original intent." He chuckled. "Problem was the Christian presidents slowed things down. Said we weren't trusting God to protect His creation. They diverted the needed funding elsewhere."

"They did a lot of good."

"Agreed. We had to find other ways to fund the program." He stared down at his cup. "We did. But I haven't had to lie so much in my life."

Not sure how the general would react, Larry lightly put his hand on the man's forearm. "I know God understands. You saved as many lives as you could."

"And I know God protected those He could." Malcolm shook his head. "Doesn't make it any easier."

"Not everything is easy."

"Problem is," the general raised his eyes to the screen. "There's a lot more involved than even I knew. Secrets were so deeply buried I had no way to find them."

Frowning he asked, "Like what?"

"Like where the technology came from to power these ships. I've seen the designs on the original ones. I don't understand how, in a hundred years, we could have advanced so quickly."

"Desperation?"

"Maybe. But there's a natural progression. We seem to have missed a few steps." He sat back. "I'm not a scientist like your sister, but even I know when it doesn't add up right."

"I could toss out a counter question." Larry smiled. "How'd they make a hydrogen bomb in the nineteen forties or put a man on the moon in the nineteen sixties? The technology wasn't advanced enough to support it, yet they managed."

"With a tremendous loss of life because of accidents. There was the fire in one of the modules and I've heard some dark tales about the fates of Russian Cosmonauts." The general's fingers drummed on the table. "I take it you've heard the accusations about the first lunar landing being faked."

"I've heard it said the astronauts couldn't have survived the amount of solar radiation in the system at the time."

Borromeo sipped his coffee. "One of those historical mysteries we'll never have an answer to."

"I hope to one day." He figured he'd allow the general to stew on that for a bit.

"When we get to heaven you mean."

"Exactly."

"You're right. Thanks for the reminder."

"You're welcome."

Borromeo got up. "Good night, Larry."

Larry also stood. "Good night, Malcolm."

With a slight nod, the general left, taking his mug of coffee with him. Larry sat back down. He'd learned a lot in just a few short minutes. Enough to know things were not as they seemed.

"Lord," he prayed. "Only you know what truly lies before us. I thank You for the knowledge and wisdom we're all going to need."

~ * ~

Where had the time gone? Larry wondered as he threw the protective web over his body. The ship shook violently and he hoped Jeanie was okay. Susanna had been put in Zero G, as had the cat, just a few hours earlier. Another shudder ripped through the walls.

"God protect us." He couldn't help it. The launch out of Earth's atmosphere had been easy in comparison, even with Yellowstone exploding. Of course, it didn't help they were landing in the middle of a storm.

"No help for it," Kal had told him. "We had just enough fuel to get here. They didn't leave any margin. We have to land."

His Christian brother was on the bridge ready to take over in the event something happened to the main pilot. A loud pop sounded followed by the smell of burning ozone. Larry closed his eyes and prayed very hard. He couldn't believe God had brought them this far only to allow them to crash.

Rattling started and a moaning sound as if the metal used to construct the ship couldn't support the stress being forced on it. He put his hand on the wall only to yank it away. The walls vibrated violently.

There were several cracking noises and for some reason, his mind flitted back to what he'd heard about the Titanic. So many on that fateful night had thought there was nothing to worry about. Over fifteen hundred had died when the ship sank, including most of the crew.

"Now," he spoke out loud to himself. "No reason for such dark thoughts. God is protecting us." Had those in the past believed the same only to lose their lives?

He bounced up, even under the webbing, before his body settled back on the spongy bunk. They'd probably hit an air pocket. He remembered similar occurrences when flying with pilots or as a passenger on a hover. That's why people were encouraged to keep their seat belts on.

"Guess we're in the atmosphere." Although no one was in room with him, it reassured Larry to keep talking. His bunk mate no doubt was still in engineering and had his hands full with trying to keep the ship together.

An image drifted to the surface of his mind. He'd watched a much older show than his favorite and the engineer kept complaining, with his Scottish brogue, about what the captain was doing to his engines. He could imagine a similar scene taking place now.

"Humor, Father?" Probably to help him relax and not worry. Despite what most people thought, God did have a sense of humor. He'd learned much during his years of fellowship with the Almighty.

Larry swore he heard a ripping sound and prayed nothing serious had happened or that the ship would come apart as they set down. They needed the compartments to start the new colony, not to mention the stored supplies.

He frowned. Was it his imagination, or had the ship slowed. How he wished he could have been on the bridge this time to watch. What did their new home look like up close? Were there trees? He laughed at the unintended pun as he remembered Jack's earlier quip about them being borrowed from his namesake.

Another sound like twisting metal and a loud whistling followed. If they were still in space he'd have worried, but since they weren't, at least he didn't have to worry about decompression.

"Father, please get us on the ground." He closed his eyes and kept praying as the ship bucked, strained and screeched down.

The sudden silence made him open his eyes. Were they down? There was a slight bump before General Borromeo's voice came over the intercom. "Welcome to Galilahi, everyone. In a few minutes we'll open the main door and we can begin to disembark. I'm sure after being cooped up for several months, we'd all like a breath of fresh air." He heard laughter from the bridge crew. "If we can arrange it, we'll have a big picnic tonight to celebrate. Since actually setting up the colony will take some time, plans are to start tomorrow. If all department heads will report to Lin Dragoon immediately, she'd hand out tomorrow's assignments." There was a brief quiet before the general barked the order they'd all been waiting for, "First recon team, crack the door."

Larry pulled the web off and opened his own door. He could see a few people in the corridor. They stood there like he did—waiting.

Whooping and shouting echoed over the internal coms. Jack's jubilant voice yelled. "Thank you for flying with us. The captain has turned off the seat belt sign. Please, check the overheads for your belongings as you disembark." The young man shouted. "We made it!"

Laughter filled the hallway and the colonists began to shuffle out. Larry joined the throng, managing to find Jeanie in the process. His youngest sister smiled up at him and took a deep breath as they reached the door.

"I never knew fresh air could be so—" she didn't seem to know the word she wanted.

"Yeah." He borrowed one of her favorite words.

"Should we go get Susanna?"

He shook his head as they walked down the ramp. "It'll take Amira several hours to free her patients and check them out. Susanna will find us later." His feet touched the rust colored ground.

"Sort of like Red Rocks," Jeanie observed. She bent down and took a handful of the dirt.

"Sort of," he agreed, wondering if the ground had the iron content like the natural outside theatre near Denver.

"Doc Byers is gonna love it!" She skipped ahead and joined Jack, who greeted her with a huge grin. The two hugged, and stayed standing together with their arms around each other's waists.

The crowd moved forward and he allowed himself to join them. Finally, he stepped to the side and took a moment to examine their new home. Of course, there were trees. He was sure Jack loved that. Not the stately pines he might have expected, but shorter, bush like branches with spiky magenta needles.

From what Larry could tell, they had landed in a valley. Several kilometers away stood several rolling hills covered in vibrant colors almost like a rainbow. The sky overhead tumbled in shades of violet, navy and lime green. Sometimes he caught a zagged flash in it.

He put out his hand almost expecting to feel drops of rain. Instead a cool moist breeze sighed over his flesh. Shivering from the sensation, he wiped his hand on his pants as he remembered an overused plot line. "Hope the planet isn't alive," he half mumbled and prayed.

Chapter 14

Several weeks had passed since they'd landed and Susanna stretched as she got up from her desk. A cool breeze winged through the open tent making her shiver. Automatically she checked on her baby, who slept in a box, pulling the tiny quilt tighter around the infant. Kal had promised as soon as they finished the basic shelters he'd make her a cradle. She hoped it was soon since her daughter would soon out grow her present bed.

Susanna crossed her arms over her chest, pulling her thick wool cloak tighter and watched the activity around her. A faint mist shrouded the colony hiding some of the dull gray buildings. During the first few days the ship had been taken apart and arranged according to the basic plan which had been agreed upon before they'd left Earth.

The largest section containing the cafeteria, child care, workout gym and other group activities, sat in the very center. Not far away the infirmary and the quarters for the health care staff had been set up. Next to it was the governor's office, where Dragoon and her staff ran the colony. The rest were like spokes on an old fashioned wagon wheel, circling out and grouped together according to profession. Some of the furtherest out housed the few families who had come with them.

She'd been surprised to find out how many of her fellow colonists had been trained in professions that didn't exist anymore. They had a blacksmith who had been part of several Renaissance fairs where he'd learned and practiced the ancient art. Another who had traveled the world learning the old herbal remedies and worked beside Dr. Upala. Kal and she smiled at the memory of him telling her, had taken up wood carving and apprenticed under someone in the Rocky Mountains to learn how to make furniture.

"You're smiling," Larry teasingly accused as he ducked under the tent and rubbed his cold red hands together.

"Just remembering how amazed we all were at the variety of old crafts people had learned." She sat back down at her desk.

"Makes perfect sense." He pulled up one of the folding chairs and sat. "Most of the people for these colonies were picked years in advance. Would have to in order to get the right balance and give them time to train."

"True." She inclined her head in the direction of outside. "How's it going out there?"

"First of the crops are planted. Luckily they had the sense to stock the new hybrids so they'll grow faster."

"Will we be able to get the crops in before the colder weather starts?"

"No idea, Susanna." He blew on his hands. "I'm not a farmer."

"Could have fooled me," she bantered back.

"Just helping out. That's what a good pastor does."

"Seen Jeanie today?"

"She's at the vets being trained as an assistant."

"Least she found something she can do."

He chuckled. "Not what she'd planned to do with her life."

"She's always liked animals. It's a good fit."

"Won't argue there." Her brother got up and paced back and forth. "Aren't you cold?"

"A little, but we won't have all the comforts of home like we're used to so," she shrugged. "I'm just weatherizing."

"Why isn't Geri in day care?" He kneeled down next to the box and gently ran a finger across his niece's cheek.

"Because she's nursing and I'd spend all my time running back and forth."

"You could still run your team and keep both of you warm." He sounded almost if he was pleading with her.

She sighed. Susanna knew she understood more about the possible future of their colony than her brother. "Larry, this isn't going to be an easy life."

He gave her an odd look. "Neither would have staying on Earth." He rose after tucking the blanket tighter under Geri's chin. He stared out at the mist now turning to rain. "How many did they guess would survive the first year?"

"Depends on the harshness of the cold season, the amount of food we grow, disease." She rose and put an arm around him. "Only God really knows."

"Isn't that supposed to be my line, sis?" He smiled at her and gave her a hug.

"Sometimes even you need reminding."

"We made it this far. Guess God isn't done yet."

"That's right." She went back to her desk. Byers should be reporting back soon. The geologist had taken a team to explore some of the distant points of their valley.

"Know what's really strange." Larry again sat on the folding chair. "Since we arrived, I get the feeling we're being watched."

She glanced up at him. "There are some native animal forms. It's probably them you're sensing."

"Probably." He rubbed the back of his neck. "I know the animal handlers continue to post a night guard after we lost one of the cows."

The first night the herd had been put out one of the cows had vanished. It had been assumed one of the local predators had claimed it as prey. Odd thing was, they'd never found a carcass. That had caused a great deal of speculation among the biologists. After the incident, a closer watch had been kept on all the animals and the first newly completed structure from the odd little trees had been a barn, located close to the vet clinic.

"At least we haven't lost anything else."

"Thank God." Larry got up and headed out. "Time to go back to work."

"See you at dinner!"

He waved back at her before vanishing in the growing fog. Other buildings got swallowed up and Susanna began to feel very isolated. She turned her attention to her reports currently on her laptop. It was an older technology, but they could run them on solar batteries, at least until they wore out from age or use.

Geri began to fuss. Susanna stopped reading and picked her daughter up, careful to keep the quilt wrapped tightly around the small body. She'd been thrilled and terrified when Joyce, the pediatric nurse, had placed her baby in her arms the first time.

"It's okay," Joyce had reassured her. "Babies aren't breakable and the nice thing," she'd leaned close, "you can carry them anywhere."

Of all the advice she'd gotten, Joyce's made the most sense. Susanna had gotten used to taking her daughter everywhere with her, on short forays into the nearby woods, to dinner, and while she worked. Being close to feed and change Geri cut down on a lot of time and allowed her to do her job.

"Whampf."

Susanna started. Had she heard something? Protectively she held Geri against her and listened. The fog now surrounded them and even if she shouted for help, she doubted anyone would be able to find her.

Scratching in the dirt and inquisitive sniffing caused her heart to thud. Geri made a tiny screech and a massive lion like head poked out of the dense mist and reached its nose higher as if to get a better whiff.

Frightened for them both, she sat completely still as she'd learned from the lectures by their wildlife specialists.

'God,' she prayed silently, 'please, please, make it go away.'

Clicking noises echoed around her. The huge red-maned head made a type of huffing sound and turned to leave. Its huge body knocked over Geri's box and the sudden crack caused her daughter to cry.

"No," she squeaked, trying to quiet her baby as the beast turned to face her.

Snap, snap, crackle. The animal snarled and retreated, leaving the two of them alone.

Shaking, she stayed put for a long, long time, rocking Geri and praying for the fog to lift so she could return to the cafeteria. The constant patter of rain beat against the top of her shelter and the area grew even darker. And colder.

"Hey, Susanna!" a voice called to her. Kal appeared and she jumped up, glad to see another human being. "It's almost dinner time and we were concerned about you."

"Kal!" Her fear must have been on her face because he immediately put an arm around her.

"What's wrong?"

She told him about her visitor. Her tears fell across her cheeks finally allowing her to release her pent up fear.

"You're okay, and so is Geri. Come on." He led her out into the dark, pausing to pull her hood over her head. "We need to tell Dragoon and the general about this."

Luckily, Susanna had worn her boots so her feet stayed dry. The area was saturated and they splashed through a number of puddles. Once they reached the main building, Kal helped her get her cloak off. It was soaked. He hung it up for her.

"Let's take Geri to day care," he suggested. "Krissy will help watch over her."

She smiled. His niece had taken to her daughter from the second the two had met. A part of her wondered if it was a sign from God. She shut down that trail of thought as she wasn't ready to even think about remarrying yet.

Kal kept his hand on her arm, guiding her through the gathering colonists. When they reached the day care, he waved at one of the attendants who rushed over and took the baby. "We'll be back sometime after dinner," he said. The girl nodded and disappeared inside. "Geri will be fine, Susanna." He gently urged her away. "After dinner we'll track down our leaders."

They ended up at table near the edge of the room. Larry found them, as did Jeanie and Jack. Minutes later Amira joined them, and Susanna wondered why the doctor's plate was heaped full.

Amira must have seen her questioning look. "Missed lunch," she explained as she sat down next to Larry.

"Should have let me know, I would have brought you something." Her brother gave Amira a smile. Susanna recognized that special smile she'd often gotten from her husband. She sniffed trying to fight the overwhelming urge to cry. Instead she examined the pair trying to decide if the two of them had figured out how they felt about each other yet.

"You were busy," the doctor returned. "I know we have to get the crops planted."

Kal twirled his fork in his food. "I didn't think, from all the reports I'd read, Galilahi got so much rain."

"Unfortunately," Susanna spoke up. "They make the reports based on a single fly by and a brief exploration mission."

"Oops! So sorry! You landed in the middle of an ice age?" Jeanie grinned at her joke.

Jack pitched in. "You lost what during a storm?"

"You can't get home you say?"

Susanna decided to put a stop to their antics. "Enough you two. This isn't the time."

"Your sister is right," Larry agreed. "The first mission here could have landed anywhere." He poked a piece of meat in his mouth.

Kal lowered his voice. "Susanna had a run in with some sort of animal this afternoon."

"You and Geri okay?" Larry reached over and took her hand.

"I'm fine. A bit shook up."

Amira frowned. "Talked to Dragoon and the general yet?"

"Planned to do that after dinner."

The doctor bit her lip like she wanted to say something but knew she shouldn't. "I've been hearing some rumors about animal sightings all over the colony. They're always accompanied by clicking sounds."

"So was mine."

"Make sure you tell them that." Amira glanced down, then back up. "I have the strangest feeling we're not alone here."

"There are animals," Jack pointed out.

"Isn't what I meant." Amira pushed her half empty plate away. "The clicking sound, to me at least, means the animals were controlled by something intelligent."

"Yeah, right." Jack slumped in his chair. "Humans are the only intelligent species in the galaxy. Least that's what everybody keeps sayin'." He shot a question at her brother. "Ain't that right, Preacher?"

Larry tapped his fork on his plate. "I know the Bible says God created man in His own image and ordered each animal and even Adam, to reproduce after their own kind."

Jeanie inserted her opinion. "Maybe, Larry. But what is God's image?"

"Spirit and love."

"So, what does that tell ya?"

"You're playing word games with me." He winked at his youngest sister. "Like you did when you turned thirteen and questioned everything."

"Still do." She got up. "Come on, Jack. Let's go find the gang."

Chapter 15

Larry watched his youngest sister take Jack's hand as the couple weaved through the tables and people. Their relationship made him uneasy especially since the soldier wasn't a Christian. True, she might not have a lot of options, but being unequally yoked could cause her no end of martial problems. He knew because he'd counseled too many couples with the same stumbling block through the years.

"You're worried about her," Amira observed. She sipped her coffee and gave him a smile. "She's a smart young woman."

"Little too smart," he mumbled back.

"We can't watch over her all the time," Susanna reminded him. "We have to trust God she will make the right decision, or else we're there to help her when she doesn't. Besides," his sister leaned forward against the table, "I seem to recall we both made some bad choices in our lives."

"Part of being human," Kal added. "How does the verse go, something about God remembering we're dust?"

"It's in Psalms somewhere." Larry rested his hand on his mug of now cold coffee. "Basically means He made us, knows our nature and that we're going to stumble and goof up."

The doctor frowned as she gazed into their faces. Larry could tell their words troubled her. "You make it sound like God is forgiving if we don't follow His laws."

Larry suddenly realized this was the door he'd been waiting for. *Don't let me mess this up, Father,'* he silently prayed before he opened his mouth. "Tell me, do you think God has judged you because you haven't kept a kosher kitchen here and ate whatever was prepared, even if it wasn't prepared the way you normally would in your home?"

Amira blinked her pretty brown eyes. "I didn't have a choice."

"That's the point." He put his hand on hers and liked the way they seemed to fit together. "Even in the Old Testament, God forgave his children when they sinned and returned to Him. He didn't say, 'You goofed up and now I'm going to find someone new to worship me.'"

"That's what I've heard from Christians all my life." He heard the bitterness in her voice.

He squeezed her hand slightly. "I'm sorry. They were wrong."

Susanna reached across the table and laid her hand over his. "The Bible tells us we Gentile Christians are grafted onto the branch of Judah. Never once does God tell us we replaced the Jewish people."

"We're just added on," Kal said as if to emphasize the point.

"I've never heard it explained like this before." Amira pulled her hand away. She got to her feet. "I need to get back to work."

"I'm always here if you have questions," Larry assured her.

"You are a very unusual preacher."

"Think I remember you telling me that before."

She smiled. "And I still mean it." Leaning over she gave Larry a quick kiss on the cheek. "Later." The doctor left them.

"Love it when God does that." Susanna, her face beaming, said.

"Me, too."

Kal gave Larry a smirking grin. "Amira likes you."

"I know. I like her."

"Like her? Or, *like* her?"

Larry groaned. "Don't you start."

"Hey, what's a brother for?"

He knew Kal meant a Christian brother despite the fact he'd like to have the young man in the family. Was going to depend on Susanna of course and he doubted she was ready to find a new husband. "When were you going to talk to Dragoon and the general?"

Kal threw a questioning look at her. Larry didn't miss the slight redness in his sister's cheeks. "Susanna?"

"Are they free?" She picked up her glass and finished her water.

Both men turned in their chairs to view the table up front where the two leaders normally sat. Oddly enough there didn't seem to be anyone with the general and Dragoon except for a couple of her staff members.

"Looks like," Kal told her.

"Guess we'd better tell them then." She got up and nervously smoothed her top. Larry knew it was an old habit when she was unsure about something.

"Come on." Kal took her elbow and urged her across the room.

Larry tagged along, using the excuse to get a good look at people's faces. He read exhaustion, worry, here and there excitement, a few loving glances exchanged. There was even one person sound asleep, his head resting on the table despite the loud murmuring filling the room.

Borromeo got to his feet and greeted their group with a warm smile. "What brings you to our table?"

"I," Susanna began. "I had an encounter with a creature sort of like a lion."

The general pointed to an empty chair. She sat, as did Kal and Larry.

"Please, tell us." Borromeo sat back down.

Dragoon narrowed her eyes, but it seemed to be her only reaction while Susanna told her story. Larry got the impression their leader knew more than she was telling.

"And it left when this clicking got intense?" the oriental woman pressed.

"My feeling is it was obeying the clicks."

The general's bushy eyebrows shot up. "Intelligent control?"

"I guess."

"Not possible," Dragoon objected. "Galilahi has no intelligent life."

"Are we sure?" Larry heard himself say.

"There was nothing in the report."

Borromeo thoughtfully rubbed his jaw. "Ours was the last colony ship out. Maybe—"

"No." Their leader whacked the table top with her hand startling a few colonists nearby. "Not possible."

"But what if they had found something?" Larry's mind was churning "Time was short, that was common knowledge, and if the expedition had found an intelligent life form, maybe they covered it up or perhaps our leaders buried it, in the interest of saving human lives."

Kal nodded. "I know these missions take years to plan and execute."

"And," Susanna added her opinion. "I know my team wasn't given access to the data gathered until much later, when we should have had it from the start."

Dragoon's face darkened. "Enough. You will not speak of this to anyone." Her voice held a warning tone.

"They won't," the general promised.

Larry gazed at the general in surprise. Borromeo had always been a staunch ally. Imperceptibly he saw the black man shake his head and his dark eyes held a warning.

"If you think it's best," the pastor conceded.

Dragoon smiled as if she'd won a battle. "It is best for all concerned. Now, if you'll excuse me." She rose and left the table, her obedient staff trailing after.

"I also have duties to attend to," the general excused himself.

Kal watched the man go and turned to Larry. "What was that all about?"

"Not sure." Larry leaned closer to Susanna and Kal. "Just don't go spreading around what happened. I suspect our leaders know more than they're saying, but Dragoon won't admit it, while Borromeo doesn't seem to have a choice."

"It's not like there aren't rumors already and what if it happens again?" Susanna asked.

"I think we'll discover that when it does."

"Maybe you'd better keep a gun with you, Susanna," Kal warned her. "I'd hate to think of anything happening to you or Geri."

"Maybe you should ask Jack to accompany you." Larry sensed they could trust the young man.

"On what pretext?" Susanna got up.

The men got to their feet as well. Larry grinned. "Ask Jeanie if she has some time to join you tomorrow. That should be motivation enough for Jack."

"You're very sneaky, big brother," his sister teased him.

"I grew up with two sisters. What did you expect?"

~ * ~

The next day dawned even more drizzly and cold. Larry groaned as he rolled out of his sleeping bag and put his bare feet on the cold metal floor. Quickly he put on his boots, grabbing his thick cloak as he went out the door. Heavy freezing rain pounded his hooded head as he hurried to the main hall.

He joined the growing throng as they entered for breakfast. It wasn't his day for KP and he regretted that. At least if he had to cook he'd be inside and able to keep warm. Instead, he would be joining many others in the fields.

"Going to be a brutally cold day," Kal commented as he edged up in the line and joined Larry. "Susanna talked to Jeanie last night about what happened. Guess your youngest sister went straight to Jack afterward. I saw him escort Jeanie to the Vet Hospital and then went back to do the same for Susanna."

"She already working?"

Kal nodded. "Before sunrise." He chuckled. "She put Geri in the nursery first though. I don't think she's going to take the risk of something happening to her daughter."

"You do the same with Krissy?"

"Always. I'm working in the fields today."

"Any idea if Dr. Byers' team made it back in last night?"

The other man shook his head. "They didn't."

"That's not good."

"Tell me about it."

They finally reached the inside and moved slowly toward the buffet line. Kevin threw back his hood and shook his cloak slightly. "I smell like a wet animal."

"They're wool. What do you expect?" Larry pulled his hood off as well.

"Least they're warm."

Each man filled his plate, grabbed coffee and found an empty table near the back of the room. Larry said a quick prayer over their meal and the two fell silent as they ate. When they finished they put their dishes in the washing area and headed for the front door. The general stopped them.

"Come with me."

They followed him down the hall and into a small room. The big man made sure the door was closed before he spoke. "I talked to Susanna this morning. Dr. Byers' team found something."

Larry listened with interest not sure why Borromeo was sharing this information with them.

"What did they find?" Kal asked.

"A large cleared off area about two clicks away and what looks like a crudely built structure at the edge."

"What do they think it is?"

Borromeo walked a couple steps away and gazed out the

round hole. Thick rain obscured any decent view and Larry was curious why the general stood there looking out.

"They think it's a landing field and possibly a trading structure." He turned back to look at them.

Both men started and stared at the general in disbelief.

"But," Kal objected. "We've seen no indication of a space faring race."

"I take it Dragoon knows." The general nodded at Larry's inquiry.

"She wants to keep it quiet, despite the mounting reports of a possible intelligent native species."

"I'd heard rumors of others," Kal told him.

"So had the president." Borromeo hesitated. "I shouldn't tell you this, but as we were putting together the personnel for this ship, we got a message from one of the other colonies."

Kal's face showed his shock and anger. "I thought we never heard from them again." His tone was accusing.

"Dragoon doesn't know. I didn't tell her."

"Did anyone know?" Larry was curious, but recalled when Malcolm had deliberately not told him when he'd asked before. He wasn't sure what to think.

Borromeo glanced at Kal with a guilty expression. "Your sister."

There was a long silence as the implication set in. Kal took a ragged breath. "She was killed, wasn't she?"

"Possibly, I don't honestly know." The general looked away briefly. "I wasn't privy to every conversation."

Kal looked like a lost little boy. "Then who made the order?"

The black man took a deep breath. "Son, there's only one person high enough to make the order and not be questioned."

Kal blanched. The knowledge also made Larry want to puke. To think a fellow Christian would have a person murdered to cover up—what?

"My God." Kal sank to the floor. Larry kneeled beside him. "What could they possibly want to hide?"

Borromeo squatted down. "I don't know the entire content of the message. What I do know, is they spoke of encountering an intelligent race who helped them survive."

"Nothing else?" What they were being told was important.

"Whatever else may have been in it, it's long gone now. We'll probably never know."

"Unless they come here," Kal whispered.

Chapter 16

Shivering because of the damp cold, Susanna retreated back to her desk to re-read Dr. Byers' report. She frowned as the words leapt out at her again. *Can only surmise it is some sort of landing field for a spacecraft and a crude structure probably used as a meeting house for trade.*

Her eyes drifted upward. "We're not alone, Lord?" The prospect both frightened and thrilled her. Not just the possibility there was a space faring race, but also that the world she now lived on had a native species. "I just hope we don't make the same mistake as our ancestors did with the American Indians."

In the past United States, spreading settlers had brought disease and ruin to the native populations of the Great Plains and other regions. There had been conflicts, land wars, buffalo massacres so the Indians would starve, until eventually the government managed to force them onto reservations. It really hadn't solved the problems since the areas were undesirable by the invading pioneers. It had just created new ones and the Indian Nations had tottered at the edge of extinction.

"May we have more wisdom," she murmured. Although considering Dragoon's native country and some of injustices Susanna had heard about, she changed her wish to a prayer.

Rain began to fall hitting the tent top in a steady pat, pat, pat reminding her of Colorado storms on the roof of her parent's house. Quickly she changed her line of thought before regret and grief overtook her. She'd made the choice to come on this expedition. Susanna had to trust God to look after her parents even if she missed them terribly.

A shape ducked into her tent and shook like a wet dog. "Hey," she protested as droplets splashed against her. Quickly she wiped away any that had splattered her laptop.

"Sorry." The figure tossed back its hood. Kal grinned at her. "It's been decided it's raining too hard to work the fields today."

"Hope we don't suffer for the decision during the winter."

He winked at her. "I'll give my share to you if it comes to that."

Despite his teasing voice she caught the seriousness on his

face. "What about Krissy?"

"I'm sure you'll look after her if anything," he stopped. "No, I promised myself I wouldn't go there." He blew on his hands. "Besides, I'm sure farmers in the olden days had set backs just like us."

"No doubt." Susanna didn't know much about modern farming back on Earth.

"Sure." He grabbed the chair her brother had used the other day and sat down. "Early freezes, prairie fires, grasshoppers, blizzards, no rain." He grimaced. "Doesn't seem to be our problem."

"Too much rain?"

"You could say that." Kal hesitated like he wanted to say something but wasn't sure he should. "There have been some shallow holes dug at the edges of our fields. None of the rows were disturbed," he continued as if to reassure her. Susanna was certain he'd read the concern on her face.

"Curious," she sat down and pulled her cloak tighter around her chilled body. The dead air space filled with warmth, but it didn't dispel the damp cold.

"One way of putting it." He glanced up and frowned. "The fog is getting worse."

Following the direction of Kal's gaze through the partially opened flap, she agreed. The thick wet stuff shrouded the colony blocking out the various buildings and tents. In its wake a deep silence swallowed up the voices and other familiar noises. It was like the two of them were alone on the planet sharing the subtle patter of rain on the tent top.

"Rerow."

Both of them jumped and Kal was on his feet, a thick book from her desk in his hand.

Susanna released a nervous laugh. "It's just Leli."

"Thought your sister took him with her to the vet's."

"Cats have a mind of their own."

The cat stood looking at them, his tail slowly swishing back and forth. Leli lifted a damp paw and proceeded to wash it dry with his pink tongue.

"I suggest you put the book back. I might need it."

Kal stared at the volume and put it back on her desk. "Sorry."

"Comforting to know I have a defender." Her tone was warm and she hoped Kal noticed.

He grinned giving her a mock bow. "You have but to make your request, my lady, and I will ride the solar winds to defend your honor."

Leli jumping in her lap distracted Susanna from the teasing remark she'd planned. "Ugh, you're wet!"

Ignoring her, Leli kneaded her cloak as he stretched out on her lap.

"You've made a conquest."

Startled by his comment, Susanna shifted her attention from the cat to Kal. His eyes gazed at her with a light she'd only seen in her husband's. "T'was never my intention," she murmured, her face burning.

"God gives us many gifts," he answered as he gently put his cold hand on hers. "We don't always want them or think we're ready."

"I think you've been spending too much time with my brother."

"There are worse influences."

"Can't argue there."

"Have you noticed," Kal asked as he pulled the chair over so he could sit next to her, "that," he never got to finish. The odd clicking she'd heard previously started up and whompfing sounded outside the tent.

Susanna held her breath, terrified. Leli lifted his head, cocking it to one side listening. Yet, she noted the cat didn't hiss or yowl like he would if there was some sort of danger.

Kal leaned over to speak softly in her ear. "This is what you heard before?"

She nodded, unconsciously reaching for his hand. He curled his fingers round hers and the two of them sat there waiting.

Canvas flickered along one side before a huge lion like head shoved the thick fabric aside. Two clear sapphire eyes blinked at them as it lifted its muzzle and opened its mouth. Savage rows of teeth were revealed and Susanna hoped it had no intention of using them on her or Kal.

Leli made an inquisitive urping noise, leaping down. Susanna wanted to grab him, but Kal's firm grip on her hand kept her still. The ginger cat trotted over to the large feline and lifted up on his hind legs as if to get a better look.

"Erow?" Almost, it sounded like Leli asked a question.

There was a 'Humpff,' response.

Click, click, clunk, tink, tink.

The lion turned its large head in the direction of the noise. Susanna noticed the odd rainbow like streaks in its shaggy red mane. There were also a couple of braids twisted with glittering gold and silver. Long claws knifed into the soaked ground before it turned and departed the same way it came.

Susanna started to shake and was glad when Kal pulled her against him. "It's gone," he reassured her. He pressed his lips against her forehead in a soft kiss. "You're safe."

She took a few deep breaths trying to quiet her racing heart and rapid breathing. Susanna had managed to stay calm while the huge feline had been there, but now that it was gone, she couldn't stop shaking.

"Let's go see Amira," Kal suggested, helping her to her feet.

"What if it's still out there?" She pulled back not wanting to face the possible threat again.

Leli hopped over the ground, ignoring the claw marks on the ground. He darted under the same area where their 'guest' had.

"I think we'll be okay." Whether what Kal said was true or not, she couldn't tell from his voice. He guided her out into the misting rain.

"Can you find the way?" Thick fog obscured even the ground before them. She felt like they were wrapped in a smothering blanket.

Kal reached out to touch the tent behind them. "I think we go that way." He put his arm around her waist and began to slowly walk forward. Luckily when they'd begun to build the colony most of the ground had been leveled out, so Susanna didn't fear tripping.

Clink, tink, clunk.

The noise echoed eerily around them causing her to stop and look wildly around. She couldn't see anything, but a part of her sensed something nearby.

"Let's keep moving," Kal urged. He tightened his arm about her and walked a bit faster.

Ting, clink, tunk.

She stopped. Kal stumbled. "That was in front of us," she told him.

"It's just the fog playing tricks with sound." He didn't sound very certain though.

They walked forward for several minutes. Silence reigned around them as the mist changed over to a heavier rain. Susanna paused to pull her hood over her head. "I think we're going the wrong way."

"We're fine."

"Kal," she turned to him and almost couldn't see his face. She reached out to touch his cheek. "We need to find shelter and stay put." A smile touched her lips. "Think of the teasing we'll get if anyone has to come and find us."

"Would that be so bad?" He leaned down. She could feel his warm breath on her face.

Tink, tink, clank, bork.

The sound broke the mood and they took a step away from each other. His hand found hers and seemed to anchor Susanna to the spot.

"Come on," he urged, taking the lead.

Trudging on the wet ground soaked the hem of her cloak. She knew her boots were covered in mud and a chill settled in around her body.

"That shouldn't be there!" Kal exclaimed.

"What?"

He reached out with his free hand. She saw his fingers rested against the trunk of a gnarled tree. Scratch marks had bared part of it and suspicious stains marred the huge boulder positioned underneath it.

Kal looked at her shocked. "I thought we were going the right way."

Tink, tink, clank, bung, lert.

Suddenly she was in his arms frightened. Susanna was conscious of his body warmth and a faint musty male scent. "I'm sure they'll send someone when they discover we're gone." She spoke as much to reassure herself as she had for Kal.

Her thoughts drifted to Geri hoping their adventure didn't leave her daughter and Krissy orphans.

'Please, God,' she pleaded, *'don't let that happen.'*

Chapter 17

Larry wiped wet cold off his face, slowly turning his head to search the colorful alien landscape. He saw the other searchers bundled in their cloaks or military green rain slickers, each carefully surveying the area around them before moving on to the next grid. Jeanie and Jack were a few feet in front of him and he hurried to catch up.

"Don't worry," Jack said, "We'll find them." The younger man pulled on the long leash causing the Husky to blink surprised blue eyes at him. The brown and black dog refused to budge, his expression almost mischievous. His attitude reminded Larry of one he'd seen in some children's movie many years back.

"Tell me again why we brought the dog?" Jeanie grumped. She huddled in her damp brown cloak looking tired and miserable.

"Because his owner said T could find anything in cold weather."

Upon hearing his name the Husky trotted over and wagged his busy tail hopefully. Jeanie's hand darted out from under the wool and scratched behind the pointed ear. His sister always had a soft spot for animals.

Jack's radio crackled and he pulled it from the inside pocket of his coat. "This is Lewis."

"Any sign of them?" General Borromeo's voice inquired.

"Not yet, sir."

"Well, keep searching and ignore any instructions that may come from Dragoon."

"Sir?"

"Just do what I ask Corporal and that's an order."

"Yes! Sir!"

Replacing the radio Jack shrugged. "Have no idea what that's all about."

Jeanie frowned. "Dragoon wouldn't really call off the search would she?"

"No idea." The corporal tugged on the leash. "Come on. Do your stuff, T."

Larry fell in behind the younger couple. He watched the dog

nose various tree trunks, clumps of stiff yellow feathery grass, and whatever else seemed to catch the canine's attention. T stopped to take a whiff of a large boulder and yipped, dashing in a tight circle to hide behind Jack's legs.

"What in the world?" The young soldier glanced at the cowering dog and back at the rock.

"One of our lions maybe." Larry squatted down to take a look at the mud. He wasn't much of a tracker, but he remembered some of his basic survival training. The dog's tracks were clear since they were fresh. There were some faint larger paw prints and what looked like maybe two different boot sizes. "I think they came this way." He straightened automatically checking out the landscape ahead of them.

"They leave tracks?" Jack had managed to coax the dog next to him and was rubbing T's head.

"Possibly." He blew on his cold hands. "Susanna and Kal might have taken refuge in a cave up there." Larry pointed upwards at the jagged line of rocks on top of the hill they'd have to climb.

"But wouldn't they have come back after the rain stopped yesterday afternoon for a couple of hours?" Jeanie asked concerned.

"Only one way to find out." He headed up the incline. His sister and Jack followed with T trailing behind.

They climbed not talking for a long while, the rain falling around them, the sound reminding Larry of walks in the forests back home. Familiar yet alien on a world so far from Sol's bright warmth and Earth's blue sky.

"More tracks here." Jack's comment interrupted his thoughts.

"They don't look like boots." Jeanie's observation caught Larry's attention and he eased back to where the couple had stopped.

"No, they don't," the soldier agreed.

He examined their find. Some of the feathery grass had been smashed into the mud. Mixed with it were large animal like impressions, but not the same as the paw print he'd seen by the boulder. "New guests to the party."

"Oh, I hope Susanna is okay." Jeanie shifted back and forth from one foot to the other. He knew she was either worried, cold, or both.

The two men's eyes met. "We need to go on," Jack said.

"Agreed." Larry started to take the lead again.

"I'll take point."

He waited as Jack squeezed past him on the narrow trail, if it was indeed a trail. The younger man handed the leash to Jeanie as he passed her. "You stay between us," he instructed.

"Yes, sir!" she replied mockingly.

Continuing to ascend the ever increasing steep path, Larry wondered if they were going in the right direction. How could his sister and Kal Devon have navigated this path in the rain and dense fog they'd had three days ago?

"Father, I hope they're safe," he muttered under his breath.

T perked up his ears and wagged his tail. The Husky probably thought Larry had been talking to him. He ran a hand over the damp fur.

Fog crept back in obscuring their back trail. T made his funny squeaky growl, nervously pulling at the leash Jeanie held.

"What's wrong with you?" She stopped and pulled the leash in. T tried to pull away but she jerked gently. "No."

"Guess he doesn't like the fog either." Jack had stopped to allow them to catch up. "I can see what looks maybe like caves."

"Sure they aren't just cracks?" Jeanie gave Jack a grin.

Larry shook his head. He counseled many couples who were acting like they did. It was as if, at this moment, no one else in the world existed but the two of them.

"Very funny," Jack retorted, landing a kiss on Jeanie's mouth. "Now, hush. I don't want you scaring anything."

"T will do that for us," she joked back.

A movement caught Larry's eyes distracting him from the couple's antics. "Did you see that?"

"What?" Jack's attention immediately shifted to the rocks above.

"I thought I saw something move." He was sure he'd seen a shape dart around one of the upright rocks and disappear into a crevice beside it.

"I'm sure those lion things have prey. I'd bet that's what you saw."

Larry frowned. "I'm not so sure. I think it had two legs."

"Maybe it was Susanna or Kal." Jeanie took a step forward. "Come on you two, let's get up there!"

"Stay behind me," Jack ordered again. "I want you to be safe."

"This is my sister we're talking about. I will not just stand here while you two *Men* decide whether it's safe for little ole me to go up there."

"I know that tone," Larry explained, trying not to laugh at the puzzled expression on the soldier's face. "We'd better get up there or Jeanie will beat us both there."

"You bet I will!" She stamped her foot and glared at Jack. "Well?"

The younger man shrugged. "If you insist." Jack took point again, sliding his handgun out of its side holster.

"Oh, that'll make a great first impression," Jeanie mocked, "meeting a new race with a weapon in hand. Or at the very least, you'll scare my sister and Kal half to death."

"Don't you know how to be quiet," he hissed back.

"Jeanie," Larry interrupted before she could say another word. She glared at him but kept silent.

The path suddenly evened out and they climbed up what looked like black stone stairs. To his eyes they didn't look hand hewn although they seemed to be both smooth and uniform. T's nails clicked as the dog followed.

"Ruins?" Jack glanced back.

"No idea."

When they reached the top there was more trampled grass and a mix of tracks. Larry tried to peer through the thick fog. He could only see shadowy lumps he assumed were the rocks they'd seen below.

Jeanie screeched and grabbed at a tuff of fabric stuck in a rock. "This is from Susanna's cloak."

"I'd better call this in." Jack extracted his radio. "Base this is Lewis."

Static whistled and Larry wondered if they were now out of range.

"Base this is Lewis."

More high pitched static replied.

"Anyone, this is Lewis."

No answer. Jack frowned. "Maybe we should go back down and get help."

"And what if Susanna and Kal need help?" Jeanie tossed a

desperate expression at both of them. "We can't just leave!"

"We are already here," Larry ventured. His sister had a point, but so did Jack.

T growled although his ears were back and he'd tucked his tail between his hind legs.

"We've got company," Jack said quietly. He released the safety on his gun.

Jeanie glanced around them. "I see only fog."

"Shhh, sis." Larry could sense it, them, too.

The fog seemed to grow thicker, swallowing up any sense of direction. Clicking bounced eerily seeming to come from everywhere. T huddled on the ground whining. Larry knelt down to try and comfort the dog.

"Now what, Lord?" he whispered. A clear picture formed in his mind. Right in front of him was a patch of ground and beyond, a cave. Without thinking he took Jeanie's hand and ordered, "Follow me."

He heard his sister gently urging the Husky to follow.

"Where are you going?" Jack demanded.

"God's shown me the path of escape."

"Yeah, right," the soldier muttered, even as he fell in behind the two siblings, covering their retreat with his weapon.

Placing one trusting foot in front of the other, Larry followed the silent instructions. He put his free hand out in front of him in the case of an unexpected obstacle, like the creatures currently surrounding them yet who hadn't attacked or approached them.

His hand finally met slick wet rock. He felt along the surface until he found the edge of the opening. "This way." Larry stepped inside. Where there should only have been darkness, faint light lined the rough walls. There seemed to be an abrupt left turn and he stopped before going further.

"Wow." Jeanie reached up to touch the light. "Think this is natural?"

"I don't see why not. Jack, any sign of pursuit?"

"No." He lowered his gun but didn't put it away.

"I wonder where this goes," Jeanie said. His sister started to move around him, T oddly enough not resisting.

"Don't!" Larry grabbed her. "Caves have their own traps." Memories of the many tours he'd taken back on Earth darted through his mind. There could be bottomless pits, underground rivers which could sweep them away, mazes they could get lost in.

A loud clack sounded outside the entrance. Instinctively the three edged further into the cave. A whumpfing noise announced the presence of something. The dog whined again trying to hide behind Jeanie's legs. Jack braced his weapon tightly with both hands, aiming it at the fog covered hole.

"Rerow."

Larry started and turned to look behind them. Standing on four paws was a ginger tabby who looked very much like Leli. Its tail swung slowly side to side and it blinked yellow eyes at them.

"Leli!" Jeanie shouted and knelt down to scoop up the cat. The feline darted back probably because of the dog.

"Are you sure?" Larry asked his sister.

"I know my own cat."

Leli turned his head as if there was something behind him. "Rerow," he prompted again taking a few steps toward the turn, pausing as if waiting for them to follow.

"This feel like a trap to anyone else?" Jack edged along the stone wall still watching for their unseen menace.

"More like herding." Larry didn't sense they were in any danger however. Rather, something important was about to happen.

"I think we should follow Leli." Jeanie glared at them and faced the cat. "Where to?"

The feline disappeared around the sharp turn. His sister followed, T trotting obediently behind. Larry took a deep breath. "Come on, Jack."

Grumping under his breath the younger man darted around, his weapon up in case of danger. Instead, the trio found themselves in a large cavern so high Larry couldn't see the ceiling. His nose picked up the faint burning smell similar to wood fires he'd known but different. It had a slightly sweet odor.

At the far end a group of figures huddled. Leli boldly strode across the area and announced himself. They turned and he heard Jeanie gasp as she took several steps backward. T tugged against his leash, his bushy tail wagging wildly.

"Larry," her voice held an uncertain note.

"Put your gun away, Jack." T's friendly behavior seemed to indicate they weren't in any danger. "If they meant to hurt us, they would have already." Larry walked forward with more courage than he actually felt. "Hello."

The tallest and biggest of the group agilely walked down some sort of natural stairs on its hind legs, though its long, slender tail never touched the rock. It cocked its huge leopard like head and sniffed. A soft growl escaped the teeth laden mouth.

"Urrrp." Leli interjected.

Large golden brown eyes shifted to his sister, glanced down at the Husky, then swung back to survey him. Its mouth opened again except instead of an animal sound, as he'd expected, words issued forth. "God told us you were coming," the soft, oddly accented voice said. "Tell us of His son."

Chapter 18

The rain had finally stopped, but the heavy fog prevented any attempt to leave the safe haven the pair had found. Susanna stood at the cave entrance, hugging her cloak tighter against her chilled body. Dampness clung to the wool and she wished they were back at the colony. At least the unseen menace they'd been fleeing from seemed to have given up.

"Morning," Kal sleepily greeted. He ran a hand through his hair and grimaced. "I could really use a shower."

"Rain's not good enough?" She gave him a teasing smile.

"No soap."

"One more thing we'll have to learn to make." With a quick glance at the dismal weather, Susanna retreated back into the cave interior. She sank down on a rock and put her face in her hands.

"God is looking after us," Kal said as he knelt beside her. His hand rested on her shoulder and she was glad of the comfort he was trying to offer. "We have fresh water and at least the funny fruit we found isn't poisonous."

"True." She gulped attempting to hold back her tears. She desperately missed her daughter, her brother and sister. "Just very bitter."

"Maybe I should propose while I'm down here."

"What?" Raising her head she stared into his eyes.

"I love you, Susanna. I have for a long time. I'd like you to be my wife."

"This isn't the time."

"It's the perfect time." Kal rose and sat on the rock beside her. "Just look at the setting." He motioned with his hand.

She had to admit the cave was pretty. Rusty red mixed into black with some white veins running through it decorated the walls. Not far away a triangle shaped stalactite dripped water into a clear pool. The steady drip, drip, drip had been the music Susanna had fallen asleep to every night they'd sheltered here.

"I guess we should be grateful to God for such a lovely haven." Slowly she reached out and took Kal's hand in hers. He squeezed hers gently. "I hope you'll understand if I say I need some time to think."

"Larry told me you loved your husband very much."

"You two been talking behind my back?" Susanna didn't mind really. She wished her husband had also been good friends with her brother.

"I wouldn't woo you without his permission." He flashed a little boy grin at her. "I'm old fashioned."

"You're the perfect gentleman." And he had been. A facet to his personality which endeared him to her and she realized his respect for her person during the past few days was not something she would have gotten from many of the men in the colony.

Skittering stone from outside brought them both to their feet. Kal quickly moved in front of her in a protective gesture she recognized and found, to her surprise, she enjoyed.

"Who's there!" he demanded.

Bright light flashed inside and she raised her arm to protect her eyes. A soft male voice addressed them in a language she didn't understand. It didn't sound like any Earth tongue she knew and Susanna suddenly was afraid.

"We don't understand." She heard Kal's uncertain tone in his response.

"Sorry," the unknown man replied, lowering the light so it wasn't in their eyes. "Didn't realize you spoke the language of the new colonists."

"You've been to our colony?"

Had they missed the first contact meeting with a new race of beings? Susanna hoped not, still, if the stranger knew their language, it meant they had.

There was a brief silence. "Nor did I know your people had landed here."

Susanna moved to stand beside Kal. "You haven't been to our colony then." That made her both glad and nervous.

"I have met others like you on many of our trade worlds."

So! That had been a trade structure her team had found! Unfortunately it meant there were native inhabitants and the exploration team had missed them.

"If this is one of your trade worlds," Kal said, "then there must be people living here."

The man gave him an odd look. "The Charon live here."

"Charon?"

"They are people, but not like you."

"More primitive?"

"No."

Susanna suddenly understood. "You mean they aren't human."

"That is so."

"Look," Kal again took her hand. "We're lost. Could you help us?"

"I could take you to our ship. From there, we can search for your colony."

"Then you're not alone?"

"I'm with others of my family." He headed for the entrance, "Come."

They looked at each other silently agreeing it was their only hope of rescue. Susanna hurried to catch up, with Kal slightly ahead of her. Once outside in the thick wet fog, the stranger looped a vinyl like rope around their waists. For a frightening moment, she wondered if they were prisoners.

"So we don't get separated," their rescuer said as if he'd read her mind. "This way."

"Wait!" She grabbed his dark clad arm. "What is your name?"

Amusement flashed in his oddly shaded violet eyes. "I'm Hedron T'Ganth."

"I'm Dr. Susanna Gates. This is Kal Devon."

Hedron dipped his head slightly in what she assumed was either a greeting or an acknowledgement. "My Uncle will be most interested in how you came to be here. The Charon are not ones to willingly share their world."

"We didn't know they were here."

"It could go badly for you then." He tugged on the rope and they trudged through the swirling mist.

Sometime later after they'd been walking for what seemed a very long time, Kal asked her quietly, "Can you see?"

"No, but our guide seems to know where he's going."

"I don't see how he can know where he's going when we don't."

"Hedron," she called. "Do you know where we are?"

"Yes." He moved around a ledge, pulling them after him.

They entered another cave. In slots along the black walls small globes illuminated the large cavern. Parts of it seemed to glitter and Susanna realized she was looking at either crystals or diamonds.

Kal stopped. "I thought you were taking us to your ship?"

"Later." Hedron unlooped them and waved at the accommodations. "There's trading to be done."

A figure emerged from the back area. From the graceful way it moved, Susanna guessed it was probably a woman. Her guess was correct when the other joined them.

"We have guests," Hedron informed his companion.

"Welcome." The woman's voice was musical with a slight clipped accent. "I am Naomi T'Ganth." Pale fingers brushed back russet tinged hair. She turned questioning eyes at the man. Susanna noticed her eye shade was similar to Hedron's.

"They were lost. I found them just where you said they would be."

Hedron's comment surprised Susanna. She could see from Kal's expression he was suddenly wary.

"Come," she beckoned them to follow with a movement of her hand. "I am certain you are hungry and thirsty." She lowered her voice and aimed it at Hedron. "Something you should have done when you returned."

He shrugged. "Your gift is one of hospitality, cousin. Mine is otherwise."

"To each of us our own talents." Her full lips offered a smile. "Come, you look chilled. I have prepared a warm meal."

Naomi whirled like a ballet dancer Susana had once seen and led them to a ledge already laid out with bowls filled with steaming contents. The smell reminded her of roast beef stew with a hint of cinnamon and nuts.

"You were expecting us then," Kal said as they sat on flat topped boulders, each with a bowl in front of them.

"Yes," Naomi answered.

Susanna frowned. "But how could you? Hedron didn't know what language we spoke until Kal said something."

The other woman blinked. "I knew only where to tell my cousin to look."

"But how?"

Hedron spoke up. "To each of us our gifts. That is the way of it."

The way they kept repeating about gifts reminded Susanna of

passages in the Bible when it talked about what God gave to each person, the church and through the spirit.

"So you also believe in the All Knowing One."

"What?" Susanna didn't think she'd voiced her thought aloud. "You did not."

"You're a telepath." Kal leaned forward and looked into Naomi's oval face. "We've only read about such things in Science Fiction books."

"So such is not a common thing for you."

"It isn't," Susanna agreed. "And if you don't mind, I'd rather not have my thoughts read. It's rude."

"I meant no offense."

Hedron put down the cup he'd just drank from. "They are young. A fact you need to remember."

"Agreed." She picked up her mug and held it in the air. "To new friends and fair trading."

Hedron did the same with his. Susanna and Kal did as well.

"You understand," Kal said before they drank, "that we don't speak for the entire colony."

A look shadowed Naomi's face. "You speak for more than you think."

~ * ~

Susanna opened her eyes. The globes on the wall were dimmed probably to simulate night and the cave was silent. Slowly she sat up hugging the warm silk like fabric. Though not exactly cold, it wasn't warm either and she shivered where the cool air met her back.

"Can't sleep?" Kal quietly asked from his place nearby.

"It isn't that." Susanna wasn't really certain what had awoken her. She wiggled her foot and felt something heavy draped over her ankle. "What?" Slowly she reached down afraid they'd perhaps been shackled by their hosts while they slept. Her fingers encountered soft fur and a small warm body. "Well, hello."

"Erruh."

"That sounds like a cat," Kal said.

"I think it is." Caressing the small head she laid back down. That explained why she'd woken up. "I haven't had a cat around for a couple of days. Must have surprised me."

Kal moved closer, slipping his arm under her neck. She allowed the gesture thinking it would nice to have a husband to cuddle next to again. Susanna relaxed in the warmth of Kal's body and fell asleep, wakening as the globes came fully back on.

"Morning."

She turned her head to look at the man next to her. Susanna could see the uncertainty in his eyes. "Morning," she greeted back.

In the background were sounds and they both sat up. Naomi worked around the ledge table, setting out implements and what looked like bowls of fruit. Hedron didn't seem to be around.

Getting up they both washed up as best they could from a small spring trickling out of the rock wall after using the facilities they'd been shown the previous night. It was much more comfortable than using nature as they'd had to during their time in the cave.

"Good morning," Susanna greeted as she joined Naomi.

"Fair day," the other woman responded. Today their hostess wore her hair up secured with a sprig of some sort of plant. Her long heavy dress was a forest green and Susanna would have bet it was very warm.

"I don't see Hedron."

"He has gone to see if the Charon wish to trade today. In their culture, it is the males who run the errands."

"Interesting." Kal sat down on one of the boulders.

"If they come to trade," she looked at Kal, "It would be better if Susanna were sitting and you at her feet."

"Excuse me?" the two said together.

"It is the females who hunt and lead. Males are there to do their bidding."

Susanna shook her head when Kal opened his mouth. "Thank you for telling us. We wouldn't want to interfere with your business."

She couldn't understand why her comment seemed to surprise Naomi. "Thank you for your understanding."

"You're welcome. Is there any way I can help you?"

"The food is prepared. Please," Naomi sat down, "eat. If they wish to trade they will come soon."

In silence the three ate a meal of sweet and sour fruit, some sort of nutty bread, and a brisk hot beverage reminding Susanna of cranberries and milk. When they finished she helped the other woman clean up.

"I think perhaps you would both like to bathe and have a change of clothes."

"Thank you again." Susanna had been in her clothes for several days and knew she smelled.

Naomi dug clothes out of a trunk, and instructed them on how to use an odd cylinder device to bathe. She then left them in a back chamber.

Susanna glanced at Kal and he said, "I'll wait out here until you're done."

She gave him a grateful smile, cleaned up and slipped on a dress similar to Naomi's. The fabric was warm, as she suspected, and oddly soft. The color was the same as Naomi's with long sleeves and a high neck. Susanna also cleaned her hair and stepped out. "Your turn."

Kal winked at her and went into the back room. Susanna went in search of Naomi and found the trader placing various items on the ledge table.

"Hedron says they will trade today. I am making ready."

She noticed Hedron near the door as if watching.

"How soon before they come?"

"Soon." Naomi finished her preparations and sat down. "Please, sit."

Susanna did. "What should I do?"

"Say nothing. They do not know you."

Kal joined her and rubbed her shoulders while they waited. Suddenly Hedron hurried over and sat at his cousin's feet. Kal groaned but did the same. Out of the corner of her eyes, she noticed a tawny cat about the size of a bobcat jump up on the table and promptly sat on its haunches.

"I met your cat last night."

"Not a cat," Naomi said.

Before Susanna could ask what she meant, the trading party entered the cave. They were led by a tall and what looked to her like a proud white tiger on two feet. None of them wore clothes and their tails swung gently behind them. Nor did she see any type of weapon and wondered how they hunted.

Naomi rose to her feet and inclined her head. "Fair day."

The leader opened its mouth as if to speak but instead inhaled. Her large head turned to stare at Susanna and Kal. "Not your blood."

"They are not," their hostess agreed.

"Intruders!" the Charon snarled and flipped long sharp claws open.

Susanna's heart sped up. At least now she had an idea on how they hunted!

Chapter 19

"You've got to be kidding me." Jack shook his head for the umpteenth dozenth time. T lay beside the young man, the dog's tail constantly wagging.

Larry paused in his story telling. He wasn't sure how long he'd been talking. Had it been mere minutes or several hours? The small group he'd begun speaking to had grown to fill the entire cavern. Because they didn't wear clothes it was easy to tell the females and males apart. He was also surprised by the number of young, was children the right word?

At some point Leli had crawled into Jeanie's lap and this had caused an awed stir among the leopard people. They'd presented his sister with a slab of raw meat. Her expression had been priceless as Larry had watched her debate on how to politely refuse without insulting them. Luckily, Leli had solved the problem by licking the offering. It had seemed to appease their hosts.

"What do you find so unbelievable?" Larry asked the younger man. The pastor took a sip of water from the canteen he carried.

"How could creatures on another planet know anything about a god worshipped on Earth?"

Jeanie stretched. "I told you God was big and had created the universe." She waved her hand. "There's your proof you kept asking for."

"I guess." Jack fell silent.

"There is more?" their leader inquired.

"Much more," Larry answered. "More than I can tell you in a day."

"Then stay as our honored guests, Messengers of God."

"I don't think," Jack began.

Jeanie reached over and grabbed his arm. "Don't."

"Thank you." Larry got to his feet and almost fell. His foot had fallen asleep. He rolled the ankle trying to get the blood flowing again so the tingling would go away.

Their hosts politely waited, he noticed, as the group got up. The female he suspected was the leader led the way further into the cave.

"They walk like Leli," Jeanie commented. She held the cat in her arms.

Jack frowned. "Whatdaya mean?" He tugged at the dog's leash. T had stopped to sniff at something on the wall.

"Every move is deliberate, like they're conserving energy."

Now that his sister mentioned it, Larry could see what she meant. He knew cats basically walked on their toes, even if humans thought of their paws as feet. A feline's entire skeletal and muscle structure was made for balance, hunting, and grace.

"God used the same design." Larry found himself caught in a moment of wonder. How absolutely awesome was the Creator of the Universe!

"Pretty marvelous, huh," Jeanie smirked.

Jack rolled his eyes. "You're not gonna let me forget this are you?"

"Nope.

Larry smiled. Jack may not be a Christian yet, but his younger sister was a good match for the soldier.

"Here." The leopard-like feline had stopped and it was the first time Larry noticed she rolled the r.

"Thank you." He walked past their hostess into a side room. The walls were a rich black with veins of white marbling. Bunched on the floor were mounds of yellow grass, though much longer than what they'd seen on their climb up the mountain.

"A bit chilly," Jeanie complained. She loosed Leli who promptly claimed the center of one of the mounds. He kneaded for a few minutes before lying down. The cat blinked his yellow eyes at them and promptly began washing his paw.

"Least someone is happy." Jack glanced around and secured the dog's leash around a stalagmite. "Stay," he needlessly ordered.

Larry glanced back and noticed their hostess was gone. He guessed it meant they were trusted. Either that or perhaps the leopard people thought they wouldn't be able to find their way out.

"Anybody hungry?" Jack pulled a ration bar out of his pocket.

His sister made a face. "A granola bar has more flavor."

"Might be all you get."

Two what seemed to be younger leopards glided in, each carrying some type of ceramic black marbled bowls. "For you," one said extending the offering.

Visions of more raw meat danced through Larry's head and he wondered how to politely refuse. To his surprise, one bowl held some sort of reddish-blue berry and the other a steaming brew reminding him faintly of tea.

Jeanie stepped forward. "Thank you." She took one and her brother the other.

"Bring meat for furred friends." The pair scampered out with a flick of their tails.

Jack pulled some of the grass off the mounds and made seats on the dirt packed floor. First they put the meal down and then sat. Larry and Jeanie bowed their heads in a silent prayer of thanks before dipping their hands into the berries.

"Shouldn't eat that," Jack said, even as he helped himself.

"Better than those ole dry rations," Jeanie shot back.

"Not bad." Larry took another handful. "Sort of reminds me of cherries only a bit more tart."

One of the leopards reappeared with two slabs of meat. It offered one to Leli and gave the other to T. The dog promptly gobbled it down.

"What that?" Large brownish gold eyes looked at Larry.

"T is a dog."

"Think?" The young female touched her paw to the side of her head.

"Not like you and I. It's a pet."

"Not know pet." From somewhere outside a deep roar sounded. "Must go." She hurried out.

"Interesting," Jack observed.

"I'm taking it as a good sign." Larry lifted the other bowl and drank the warm fluid. Setting it back down, he continued, "They're curious about us."

"How's that old saying go, curiosity killed the cat."

"They at least knew to feed us berries and not raw meat."

"And they spoke our language," Jeanie added. "Now that makes me curious on how they know English."

"Got ourselves quite a mystery." Jack wiped his juice stained mouth with his shirt sleeve. "I'll take first watch."

"You don't think they'd harm us?" Larry was appalled at the idea.

"I think we're dealing with an alien species we know nothing about. I'd rather be safe then suddenly find myself the main entrée."

~ * ~

Faint scratches caught Larry's interest and he poked his head out of their room. Several very young leopards scurried away. He wondered if they'd been spying on them and he smiled. Their curiosity made them seem more—human.

Larry went back and sat on the grass bunch he'd earlier been asleep on. His sister had chosen the one near the wall and was curled into a ball, her cloak tucked tightly around her body. Leli had moved from his earlier bed and stretched himself along her back. He allowed his gaze to drift to the soldier. Jack slept with his arm over his eyes, but his gun hand was near his weapon. T raised his head and wiggled his tail hopefully.

Not able to resist, he tiptoed over and slid the lease off the rock. The Husky obediently followed him back to his bed and crawled in next to him. Larry scratched T's head.

Somewhere close by water dripped into what sounded like a pool. Echoing splash kept him company through his watch as did talking with God.

Well, here we are, Lord. Obviously you knew we'd arrive here one day, although how they know about You is a mystery.

Not that the Bible wasn't full of unexplained mysteries. Larry knew archeologists and historians had many times tried to explain away the miracles of God by saying it was some sort of natural occurrence. For example, a volcanic eruption might explain Sodom and Gomorrah. He chuckled. When he finally got to heaven he wanted to know what the behemoth was in the book of Job. It didn't sound like an elephant but rather a dinosaur or sea dragon, despite the fact history seemed to indicate they were extinct or didn't exist.

Except the crocodile and a few others that are still around. Are they still around? Or did they die off when Yellowstone blew, Father?

Larry shivered at the thought. The fact his parents and many others he'd known could now be dead was a sobering and almost frightening thought. He missed them terribly but he'd known when he'd agreed to part of this expedition he wouldn't see them again until he reached heaven.

Life isn't always fair is it, Lord? He shifted on the grass. T lifted his muzzle before putting it back down between his paws. *Sometimes there are sacrifices we have to make in order to allow Your will to be done.*

The dog's warmth began to penetrate the slight chill Larry had been aware of but ignoring. He lifted the end of his cloak and put it over T meaning to leave the dog's head out. Instead, the Husky burrowed under the edge and didn't move.

"Have it your way." Larry chuckled as the wool cloak settled over T's entire body. He had to admit it was much warmer this way. He ran his hand over the dog's spine before bracing his back against the stone wall.

Splat-splish-splat echoed. It was such a soothing sound Larry had to struggle to keep from falling asleep. He repeated every verse he'd ever committed to memory and even resorted to recalling recipes he'd prepared to keep him awake.

He heard Jeanie groan as she shook herself awake. Leli protested with a 'rerowww'. His sister laughed. "Sorry, you silly ole cat."

Larry glanced over at her. "Go back to sleep," she told him. "I'll watch for awhile."

"You don't have to."

She shrugged. "Wouldn't be fair to put *all* the burden on you two." Jeanie pulled her legs up and snuggled into her cloak, tossing her hood over her black hair. "I'll do my shift."

He knew better than to argue with her. Larry fluffed up some of the grass into a semblance of a pillow and scooted down into it. T shifted closer to him and he drifted off to sleep only faintly aware of the combined slightly wet dog and sweet musty scent.

When Larry woke up, he carefully stretched, feeling his muscles protest at his movement. Slowly sitting up he glanced around their cave room. His brain dimly registered four brownish red bowls, a faint growling sound and Jeanie's scolding voice.

"What's going on?" he asked.

"T tried to take Leli's breakfast." She tossed a slice of meat at the dog who was back to being tied up on the stalactite. A smaller piece she gave to the cat. The feline nibbled at it. "They left us some sort of mushy stuff and more of that odd tea of theirs."

He frowned. "Where's Jack?"

"Looking for a bathroom."

"Oh." Larry got up. "Any idea if he found one?"

"Nope." Jeanie sat down and sipped from one of the bowls. "I'm guessing behind anything would be fine. That's what I did."

Larry laughed. "Think I'll go see if I can find him."

"Don't wander far. Hmmm. I wonder how they got this warm?"

He spared her a glance before going to find someplace to relieve himself. When he got back he found the young solider had already returned and was eating breakfast.

"It isn't bad," Jack said.

Sitting on the floor he took the final bowl. The outside was warm but not unpleasantly so. He tipped it to allow the syrupy mush to slide into his mouth. It had a nutty fruity taste sort of reminding him of mixed berries and walnuts. "Not bad."

"Thought I said that." Jack gave him an impish smile. "No sign of our hosts this morning, if it is morning."

"Maybe they're nocturnal," Jeanie suggested. "Remember all the sightings around the camp were at dusk or night."

"Wonder if they're the ones with the lion headed critters?" Jack lifted the tea bowl and drank.

"Somehow," Larry found himself saying, "I don't think so."

"We heard clicking."

"If you remember, T wasn't afraid of these Leopard people." Probably wasn't what they called themselves, but Larry needed to give them a name. "He was of whatever left its mark on the boulder."

"So maybe," Jeanie ventured, "there are more than just our hosts here."

Jack shook his head. "Scary thought if you ask me." He ran his fingers through his hair and pulled them away. "Yuck. I need a shower."

Jeanie gave her boyfriend a grin. "Love you anyway, even if you smell."

"You ain't a rose yourself."

She stuck out her tongue.

"Oh, that's real mature."

Shaking his head at their antics, Larry started at T's high pitched yelp. The Husky darted behind the stalactite, whimpering in fear. Leli darted to the door of their 'room'.

"What in?" Jeanie was on her feet, followed by both men. Larry found himself tense, like he was getting ready for battle.

A giant maned head pushed itself into the opening and 'humpfed' at them. Leli arched his ginger back and hissed.

"Knew they were too friendly," Jack complained, raising his gun and aiming it at the intruder.

Chapter 20

The Charon female moved close her sweet meat tinged breath brushing Susanna's face. A thin claw traced a path across her throat and she shivered in terror. She could die right here and join her husband. But, if that happened, she would never get to see her daughter grow up!

She sensed Kal about to get to his feet and somehow her hand found his shoulder to keep him seated. No sense in him also being killed.

"Sanura," Naomi's soft voice interjected. "It would not be best to harm the messengers of the All Knowing One. For they bring the message we have all been waiting for. "

What in the world was the Trader woman taking about Susanna wondered?

The Tiger female hissed but withdrew a step. She noticed the feline had not yet sheathed her claws.

"How can this be?" the Tiger snarled.

"We do not know His ways. And we have waited long and patiently."

"Intruders!" She twitched her claws and one of the males moved forward, dropping a piece of stiff black cow hide on the ground.

At least now Susanna knew what had happened to the missing cow. She just hoped she and Kal did not suffer the same fate!

"So the Pouto tell us." Sonura grimaced, displaying her sharp fangs.

"We didn't know," Susanna began. Naomi's sharp look silenced her apology.

"Races who are young do not know our ways. We must be patient, as you would while training a youngling."

Two clear blue eyes turned to look at Susanna as if determining the truth of the Trader's words. The ears twitched and then the claws disappeared. "That is so."

A brief silence reigned in the cave and the tension hanging there she could feel. Her fingers squeezed Kal's shoulder and he dared to put his hand over hers.

The tiger didn't miss the motion. "Mated."

"Not yet," Naomi said. "To each of us our rituals."

"Truth," the other agreed.

The feline turned her attention from Susanna and Kal. She dared to take a deep breath in relief.

"We came to trade."

"As did we," Naomi graciously acknowledged. Her hand moved to show the set out items.

The tiger inspected each item although when she came to the cat, her head dipped slightly, as if in respect, before looking at what sat on the table beyond it. Susanna found it odd but didn't dare ask.

Much later an agreement had been made. The Tiger took several rock shaped bowls and offered many varieties of plants in exchange. Naomi made a great show of inspecting each before choosing three. One were thick purple leaves, another a thick stick with a hint of a nutty fragrance and the third bright orange petals.

The tiger agreed to the trade and they piled the bowls into a rough sack made of gray-blue hide. The female looked at Susanna and blinked.

"Messengers do not come as we would think," Naomi reminded the other.

"But they have come. This is a good thing for us all."

"We have waited long."

"And we wait no more." The tiger lowered herself to squat and the others did the same, the males lying on the floor. "So, tell us messengers of the All Knowing One. What is the news of His Son? Has he come as promised?"

Right then Susanna wished she had Naomi's telepathic abilities. Were they talking about God and His son Jesus Christ? She saw the trader woman nod slightly and knew that indeed, this is what they were asking about.

"He came long ago," she said and was surprised when Naomi didn't tell her to be quiet. "During a dark time in our history before even I was born."

There was a faint purring sound and she glanced at the cat still sitting on the table. It lifted a paw, licked it and washed its face.

"He was born simply, in a manager and raised by his mother and her husband." Susanna kept talking pulling details about

Christ's life as they came to her. She wasn't her brother Larry and not really practiced at speaking to large groups about her faith. About science and its advancements yes. She was comfortable doing that.

"Then, he was betrayed and sent to die on the cross."

The tigers snarled and Naomi caught her breath. Hedron leaned forward caught up in the story.

"Then it was not as foretold," the tiger leader growled.

Susanna shook her head. "Not as thought, no. Jesus was something greater. A redeemer. He came to buy us back from our sin." She told the rest of the story. His death. His resurrection. His brief time on Earth in his new body and returning to heaven in a cloud. "And so, we still wait for His second return."

"So there is still time," Hedron whispered.

"There is time," Susanna reassured him.

"I am certain," Naomi put in, "He made a course for us."

"He did," Kal spoke up for the first time. "Susanna and I have both accepted Jesus into our hearts. We can show you how to do the same."

"Then let it be done." Naomi kneeled before them. Her action made Susanna uneasy.

"You need only to kneel to God not to us." *Oh, Father, help!* Susanna pleaded. Words came to her and she led the entire group in a sinner's prayer of salvation.

~ * ~

"You okay?" Kal asked coming up behind her as she stood in the cave entrance watching the tigers leave.

"Larry would have done a better job than me. This is what he trained for."

"You did fine." He put his arm around her and she leaned against him.

"I feel like I failed them."

"You told them what they needed to hear and now there are more followers of the King and who will go to Heaven because of you."

"I am so unworthy."

"God never gives us what we think we deserve."

"Now you sound like my brother."

Kal chuckled. "Ever considered he's right?"

"Every day." She remembered what she'd said to Larry to get him to come on this expedition and his own words about dreams being fulfilled in God's time.

"So," he kissed her cheek. "When do you think our hosts will take us back to our colony."

"I got the impression they didn't know where it was."

"Doesn't mean they won't help us find it."

She laughed. She couldn't help it. It had been a long emotional day and she really didn't want to cry. "I miss my daughter."

"You're going to see her again and the rest of our family."

"Oh?" She turned so she could face him. "Have you already decided what my answer should be?"

"You already know. I'm just waiting for you to realize it."

"Kal." She sighed, looking up into his pale blue eyes. Such love shined down at her. She hadn't seen that look since before her husband died. Lightly she ran her finger down the side of his face. "I don't deserve you."

He smiled. "Probably not, but you've got me anyway." He leaned down and she allowed him to kiss her. It was sweet and tender. "I love you."

Susanna rested her head on his chest and she could hear his heart beating. It was slightly fast. She cared about him. A lot. But enough to marry him? She wasn't certain. Not yet.

Someone cleared their throat. She pulled away from Kal.

"Forgive me," Hedorn said, "but food is prepared."

"Thank you," Kal answered. He took her hand and they followed their host back to the main chamber. Steaming bowls were again set around the odd stone ledge.

Naomi waited until they sat down before she poured them a spicy smelling drink from a long cylinder. "It was a good day of trading," she said.

Susanna cautiously sipped the beverage. It was tangy with a hint of citrus. "This is good."

"Our family makes it at Homefall."

"Homefall?"

"Where our clan makes it home," Hedron explained.

She and Kal exchanged a look.

"Then yours isn't the only clan?" Kal asked.

"We are not. There are also the V'ainth's and Talons."

"And others as well," Naomi added. "Your people will learn

this."

Kal made a face. "So much for the fantasy about an open and empty galaxy we can colonize."

His comment caused their hosts to look at each other and Susanna hoped they hadn't been offended.

"Sorry," Kal apologized. "It was something our president kept saying when this mission was being put together. He didn't know there were other beings out here."

"We were not offended." Naomi sipped the cooling soup. "Many who are young have such foolish notions."

Hedron grinned. "They quickly grow up."

A chilling thought occurred to Susanna and she had to ask. "What happens if they don't?"

"They are isolated and allowed to grow up." Hedron drank some juice. "It is best for us all."

"And safer I'd bet." Kal leaned on his elbows on the table. "For them and us."

"Tomorrow," Naomi interjected, "we leave here and go to our ship. We would most honored if you consent to join us."

"Well," Kal glanced at Susanna and she nodded, "It's not like we know the way back to the colony. We were lost when you found us."

Naomi smiled slightly. Susanna suspected their hostess hadn't forgotten.

The rest of dinner passed in pleasant conversation and they went to bed. In the morning Susanna and Kal washed up, got dressed in fresh clothes that were provided, and helped their hosts pack up what would not be staying in the cave.

"I'm surprised you leave so much here," Kal commented. "Aren't you afraid it will be stolen?"

Susanna listened with interest as she helped pack up the food supplies.

Naomi shrugged. "The Charon have little need of what we leave behind. All is here when we come to trade."

"Wouldn't happen on Earth."

"Then your people have much to learn."

"Won't argue."

As they exited the cave the sun came out and weakly shone down. The grass glistened like spun gold and the rocks were slightly slippery underfoot. Hedron slung a heavy bag over his shoulder and took the lead. Naomi followed with a lighter one, their cat draped over her shoulders.

Kal kept his hand under Susanna's arm so she wouldn't slip as they made their way between the rocks and down a well-worn path. The mud squished and made footing treacherous. Even their hosts were careful helping each other over difficult patches.

"I don't think they're married," Kal said.

"No." Susanna tugged her cloak slightly tighter. It was still very chilly and damp. "They call each other cousin and treat each other accordingly." In a way, what he said was obvious.

"More like co-workers I'd say."

She shook her head. "No. There's a sense of family. You wouldn't get a co-worker to sit at your feet or run your errands." She gave him a teasing smile. "Men just won't stand for it."

"True." He pushed aside a heavy branch. "Vegetation is different."

Susanna stopped and looked around. The trees were similar to the pines she'd known back in Colorado. They were tall, bushy, and a deep blue reminding her of a vast ocean. "It's beautiful."

"Yeah."

She looked up at Kal but he wasn't referring to the trees. Susanna blushed and carefully continued down the path. Hedron and Naomi had gotten ahead of them and she could barely see their figures.

As quickly as they dared they caught up with their hosts. Luckily, the two waited at the bottom of the hill for them.

"Thank you," Susanna said.

"You are the messengers. It would not fare well for us if we lost you," Naomi answered. The cat blinked lazily at Susanna and closed its eyes. She could see its paws flexing and a faint purr reached her ears.

"How much further to your ship?" Kal wanted to know.

"We'll be there by nightfall." Hedron rearranged his bag and set off through the trees.

Moisture clung to the branches and Susanna had to be careful not to disturb any or else it dropped like rain onto them, as Kal had found out earlier. Now he ducked his head but his brown hair was wet so he pulled his hood up.

It was silent in the woods. No birds singing. No trees swaying to the wind and missing was the whispering song Susanna had heard back on Earth. No small animals scurried away as they approached.

"One would think this is a dead world," Kal observed.

"But it isn't." She reached up but didn't touch the water laden branch. "We've seen that it isn't."

The forest cleared and beyond was a huge saffron covered meadow. Sitting not far away was a splotchy gray and green orb. A figure walked down the ramp and waved at their hosts.

"Oh, Father," Susanna breathed.

Chapter 21

Clink. Clack. Lert. Ponki.

The 'lion' turned its red maned head back, as if something was behind it. Tangled in the stringy tresses Larry noticed several yellow strands trailing down to its massive shoulder. "Whumpf," it repeated.

Several snarls reached the pastor's ears. Leli hissed again. A small figure worked its way past the intruder and clicked two claws.

"Umpfff." Their unwelcome visitor backed out.

"Sorrrrrry," the small leopard female apologized. "Pouto only currrious. Not hurrrrt."

The three exchanged glances. Larry wondered if they were thinking what he was. It was the same creature, or similar, to the ones spotted around the colony.

"Pouto?" He wondered if that was the creature's name or what they called it.

Their visitor cocked her head one side. Larry had seen Leli do that when puzzled by something. He guessed it probably meant the same thing.

"Pouto." Her paw reached out as the massive head poked back inside. She rested it lightly on the mane.

"Okay, Pouto." He looked over at the soldier. "Put your gun away, Jack."

Slowly the younger man complied, still gazing at the huge creature uneasily.

"What's that?" Jeanie walked over and reached out her hand.

"Jeanie!" both men warned.

"He won't hurt me right?" She asked their hostess.

"No hurrrt," the other confirmed.

He watched as his sister touched the mane. Her fingers traced one of the yellow strands. "What's this?"

"Many Poutos. This one ours."

"Guess that's what they call the creature," Larry said. He heard the Husky whine again. Poor dog. T was so scared. "What do you use the Pouto for?'

"Watch only."

"Like a scout?" Jack asked.

Two large gold-brown eyes blinked. "Scout?"

The soldier explained. "Someone who goes before the others to see what's there."

"Ahhh, yes. Pouto."

"So they *were* checking us out!" Jack seemed both happy and a bit angry.

Jeanie turned and faced the young man, putting her hands on her hips. "Wouldn't *you* if a bunch of strangers suddenly dropped onto your planet uninvited?"

Jack sighed. "Yeah, I guess. Just like we sent out teams to check out the immediate terrain."

"See," she replied smugly. "They did the same. Besides, no one got hurt. Maybe shook up, but that was it."

A thought popped into Larry's mind. "How many Poutos?"

He saw Jack's expression. The other hadn't thought of that.

"Many."

Jack whistled. "Means more than one leopard tribe I suspect."

"Leoparrrd?"

Larry smiled. "That's what you remind of us. There was a big cat with tawny fur, black spots and a tail."

"Ahhhh." Her paw moved to her chest. "Malia."

"That her name?" Jeanie asked.

"No idea," Larry said. "What do you call your tribe and are there others?"

She hissed. "Speak to Yoana. She tell." With that, their guest ducked out. Pouto tamely followed.

"Their leader?" Jack ventured.

"Would be my guess." Larry shivered. His cloak was warm but the cave temperature, although not as cold as outside, was still chilly. It had seeped into his bones. Vaguely he wondered if he'd ever feel warm again. Their shelters in the colony were heated— for now. What would happen when the technology failed?

"So," Jeanie spoke up, "let's go see Yoana." She bent down and scooped up Leli. The cat pushed his head against her chest and she rubbed his head. A purr rewarded her efforts.

"And what is with their reverence of Leli?" Larry wondered.

Jack tugged at his camouflage coat. "Lot's of questions but

not so many answers."

He pulled out his walkie-talkie. "Lewis to base." Static crackled.

"Maybe because we're in the cave." Larry knew many things could be interfering with communication. He remembered that much from his basic training.

"Maybe." Jack's face held a worried look. "Maybe not."

Jeanie narrowed her eyes. "What's been going on that we don't know about, Jack?"

The soldier shook his head. "Not the time."

"Jack," Jeanie pressed.

"Not now."

"Come on now. If something is going on we should know about."

"I said," Jack snapped. "Not now."

His sister opened her mouth to argue, when T broke the tense moment. The Husky bounded up and yipped, his bushy tail wagging.

Smart dog. Larry reached over and scratched behind the dog's ear. "I think we should talk about his later." His comment got a dark glare from Jack. "Right now, let's go find Yoana and see what, if anything, she'll tell us."

"Interesting, huh," Jeanie smirked. "The females seem to be leaders." She put Leli on the ground before she tucked her arm around Jack's and they left their room.

Larry walked a few steps behind the couple. T trailed behind sniffing along the black walls. He saw the cat bounce past him and catch up with Jeanie.

"Maybe we should adapt the same policy," she suggested.

"Wouldn't work." Jack worked his arm free, tucking it around his sister's waist. "I'm too used to giving orders."

"Ha! Like I'd do what you'd say."

"You'd better." Larry noted the warning tone in the soldier's voice. "If you want to stay alive on this planet."

"I'm doing just fine thank you."

Larry had to smother his smile. Jeanie had always had spunk. Their father had tried to quell her, said it wasn't proper for a polite young lady. Yet, his sister had, while not quite disobeying, managed to keep her own sense of who she was. God had made each of them unique. He was beginning to see, under their current circumstances, how their personalities were well suited for the challenge.

"Hey," he called. "You two remember how to get back to the main chamber?"

Leli yowled. He proudly walked before them, his thin tail held high. At the next junction, he turned right, gazing back at them over his shoulder.

"Well," Jeanie said. "Leli seemed to know where to go yesterday so," she shrugged.

"Great," Jack gripped. "We're trusting not to get lost to a cat."

"Hey," Jeanie jabbed the soldier's upper arm. "He's smarter then we think."

"Yeah, right."

Several confusing turns later, they once again found themselves in the large cavern. Various leopards were hurrying around, dropping black or rusty red bowls into a black and white fur bag.

Their young visitor stood to one side, her paw twisted into the Pouto's mane.

"Yoana," Malia called.

A tall female stopped, her green-gold eyes resting on Malia.

Malia spoke rapidly in a series of snarls and yowls. Yoana's ears twitched before she turned her feline gaze toward Larry. "Malia says you want to know what we call ourselves."

"We'd like too, yes," he answered.

"We are the Mosi."

"Thank you." Larry's gaze swept over the tribe. "You going somewhere?"

Yoana turned and went up the black stairs. She squatted down, her paw resting on the bag. "Traders here. We meet them at the agreed upon place."

So! Dr. Byers had been right! The area they'd found a few clicks from the colony was a trading post. Larry wondered how the general and Dragoon were going to react to the news.

"Mind if we tag along?" Larry watched Yoana tilt her head to one side.

"Tag?"

Not a word she must know. "Do you mind if we go with you?"

"Larry," Jack's tone warned.

"Oh, hush." Jeanie poked Jack's arm. "My brother knows what he's doing. Besides, they probably know the way back to the colony a whole lot better than we do."

Jack grumbled under his breath.

Yoana had not missed the interaction between Jack and Jeanie. Larry had seen the slight widening of the Mosi's eyes and her unconscious movement in her paws. One sharp claw had escaped.

"No argue with female," she hissed at Jack. She stomped down the stairs, her tail flicking in what Larry supposed was anger.

The soldier started. He gulped as Yoana approached even as his hand fell on his pistol.

"Jack, don't!" Jeanie grabbed his hand. "Please," she pleaded. "He didn't mean any harm. It's different with us, how males and females talk to each other."

Yoana stopped, her one claw slowly coming up to lightly rest under Jack's chin. "Treat with respect."

He nodded, his blue eyes resentfully gazing at Yoana.

"He's young," Larry said.

"Ahhh," Yoana removed her claw and it disappeared between her toes. "Young make many mistakes."

"Yes, they do," Larry agreed. He was relieved she wasn't going to slit the corporal's throat. He had no idea how he would have explained the incident to Borromeo.

Granted cultural misunderstandings happened, like with the White men and the Indians, but since this was a first contact situation, he knew they needed to make friends with their new allies. Somewhere down the line, they might need the help of the Mosi.

The Mosi female snarled at one of the males. He huffed back and slung the bag over his shoulder.

"We go." Yoana led the way with the humans falling in behind her and the rest of the Mosi.

"Thanks," Jack said quietly.

"Just said the first thing that came to mind." *Thank you, Father,* he added silently. "And you're welcome."

"If she would have harmed Jack," Jeanie began.

Larry laughed. "Lucky for us she didn't."

The female snaked her way through the naturally lighted tunnels. Larry could hear T's nails clicking on the stone floor.

"Wait a minute," Jeanie stopped and frantically looked behind them. "Where's Leli?"

"No worry." Malia padded forward, the cat safely snuggled around her neck. "I keep safe."

Jeanie sighed in relief. "Thank you."

A whiff of dank cold air reached Larry's nose. He hurried forward to catch up with Yoana. She stood at the entrance, the fog and misty rain drenching the grass. She opened her mouth taking a deep breath.

"Not stop for long time." She turned to face the group. From her lips escaped a series of sounds both familiar and not to Larry.

"Now what?" Jack asked.

Larry shook his head. "No idea."

Several of the Mosi turned around and went back into the cave.

"Malia, you go," Yoana ordered.

The young female stood her ground. She snarled and her tail whipped behind her. "No."

Yoana huffed a couple of times. "You growing. Very well. Come." She stepped out into the storm.

"Hate getting wet," Jack groused. He pulled up the hood on his jacket.

"Maybe you should try the radio," Larry suggested.

"Yeah, good idea." He pulled it out of a pocket and flipped the switch. "Lewis to base." Static hissed. "Lewis to base, anybody copy?"

There was loud crackling but no answer.

"Guess not." Jack replaced the walkie-talkie.

"We could still be too far away," Jeanie ventured.

"Maybe." Jack looked worried. Larry knew the soldier knew more than what they'd been told. He just had no idea what.

"Go," Yoana growled. She trotted out into the storm.

"I'm going to smell like T there," Jeanie half joked. She pulled her cloak tighter and made sure her hood was over her black hair. She tugged on the leash and the dog obediently paced after her.

Larry was about to do the same when Malia handed him Leli.

"No like to get wet," she said.

"Yeah, I know." He tucked the cat under his cloak, tossed up his hood and joined the small group loping over the damp grass and slick mud.

He noted they weren't using the same trail, if indeed it had been one, they'd followed up to the caves. Instead, Yoana guided them down a well-worn path behind the tall rocks. It was covered in mud and grassy debris.

No one spoke as they descended the hill, each he was sure, concentrating on where they put their feet or paws, so no one fell or got hurt. Or, thinking of his sister, got muddy. He had to give Jeanie credit. She hadn't complained about the primitive conditions or wanting a shower.

At the bottom Yoana stopped and turned her head side to side. Moisture dripped down the side her muzzle yet she seemed oblivious to it. Her tail tip draped daintily over her shoulder.

"Dark soon."

He had to trust her instincts. She knew her planet better than any of the humans.

"Then why'd you leave?" Jack asked. Larry could hear the irritation in the other's voice.

"Easier to evade," she growled something. He suspected there was no word for it.

"Some kind of predator?" The preacher held his breath awaiting her answer.

"Large. Dangerous. Come." She spun around on her paws like he'd seen Leli do when chasing an annoying fly.

There were suddenly huge spiked needled trees before them. Branches reached out reminding Larry of huge spider legs. He shivered at the image.

He had no idea how long they traveled under the heavy branches. The faint light they had earlier faded to dark and still Yoana did not stop. When they finally did, she helped each of them up into the trees. The branch Larry sat on bounced under his weight before calming down.

To his surprise, it was large enough to sit comfortably on. He braced his back against the trunk. Leli poked his head out before ducking back and settling on Larry's lap. The cat's warmth soothed the damp chill on his tired legs.

"Sleep," Yoana told him.

He closed his eyes but called quietly. "Jack! Jeanie!"

"On the branch above you," Jack answered.

"I'm on the one next to you with Malia and T." The dog whined. T probably didn't like being up in the tree.

"Sleep she says," Jack snorted.

"Quiet!" Yoana growled. "Time for sleep."

The tree grew quiet and Larry listened as the rain pattered down and sometimes dripped on his head. He made sure Leli was safely covered and began praying.

Father, keep us safe through the night and thank you for the new allies. He chuckled at the next thought that rambled across his mind. *And Dad, put your protective hand under each of us. I'd hate for us to make fools of ourselves by falling out the tree.*

Chapter 22

Naomi hurried toward the figure. She placed her small bag on the ramp and embraced the man who had waved to them. The two briefly separated, just long enough for the cat to jump down, before they exchanged a kiss.

"Husband?" Kal ventured.

"Would be my guess," Susanna replied.

They followed Hedron who gathered up his cousin's bag. "I'll put these in the hold." He vanished inside the circular door.

"Axel," Naomi spoke, turning to face Kal and Susanna. "These are the messengers of the All Knowing One."

His dark eyes widened, before giving them a slight bow. "I welcome you. Long have we awaited your arrival."

Susanna smiled warmly although a part of her was uneasy. She had no doubt God had set this all up long ago, but to be in the midst of seeing prophecy unveiled, as it seemed to be doing, made her feel both overwhelmed and yet honored at the same time.

"Axel is my life mate," Naomi continued. "We were bonded when we came of age."

"When is that?" Kal asked. Susanna felt his hand on her elbow and felt a bit more steadied.

"Our fifteenth winter."

"Fifteen?" Susanna was shocked. In the United States, the minimum legal age was eighteen.

The other woman shrugged. "So it has been since the Rovers chose the stars."

"I'll bet there's a story," Kal whispered in Susanna's ear.

She saw Naomi smile and nod. "We have many stories and a rich history."

"Urp." The cat raised up on its hind lings to stare up at Naomi.

"I know." She reached down and fondly scratched the feline's head. "Yours are the true keepers of all histories."

"What?" Had Susanna heard correctly? "What do you mean?"

"Nels is a Felcat." She frowned. "Do you not know them?"

"We have cats. They're pets."

"Ah," she nodded as if the meaning were clear.

A drop splatted Susanna on the head. It was followed by another. And another.

"I would be honored if you boarded our ship," Axel invited. He stepped back, making a sweeping motion with his hand.

Rain began to fall like just before a tornado back home. Susanna hastily entered the ship, Kal right beside her. Nels bounced in and vanished up a set of circular stairs. Naomi entered followed by her spouse who closed the hatch.

Inside the bottom area was brightly lit. There was a long narrow hallway with a series of closed doors on either side. In the center stood the stairs the Felcat had already used.

"You'll be more comfortable in the crew area." Axel passed them. He smelled like fall rain to Susanna, damp and leafy. He was dressed like it too, in a green jumpsuit with a gray strip down his right sleeve and pant leg.

They took the stairs up several decks, their boots ringing hollowly, before Axel swung out onto a marble like floor. He took them to a circular room where part of wall seemed to be rolled back. Susanna gazed out. Outside the blue tree ocean spread similar to a wave across the hills. It touched yellow grass reminding her of a sandy beach.

She started as Kal's arm went around her waist. "Wow," he said.

"Just what I was thinking." She rested her head on his upper arm.

"I will bring you refreshment," Naomi said from somewhere behind them.

"And I have matters to attend to." Axel also left.

The pair comfortably stood there together before Susanna shook herself. Her eyes took in the curved red couches resting against the circular walls. One odd clear protrusion stuck up in the center of the room. She wondered if it was supposed to be some sort of table.

"At least they want to make sure we're comfortable." Kal chose a couch and sat down.

"So it seems." Funny, Susanna had never even considered the possibility they might be prisoners. The shared experiences of the past few days seem to indicate otherwise. She sat down and took

Kal's hand. He squeezed her fingers. "Do you think they'll take us back to our colony?" she asked him.

He glanced toward the door. "Probably, although I'd wager we have a few detours first. I'll bet there's more than one tribe."

"You might be right." She was curious how many there might actually be.

The door swooshed open and Naomi rejoined them. She carried a pearl like platter with several intricately carved cups and bowls upon it. Susanna picked up a scent reminding her of cinnamon, chocolate and cherries.

Naomi put the platter on the clear plastic table. "I brought you something to drink and eat."

"Thank you." Susanna rose and took one of the cups. She sipped the beverage. It rolled on her tongue and tasted like it had smelled only with a slightly sweeter bite. "This is good."

The Rover woman smiled. "I'm glad you like it."

Kal also helped himself and stuffed his hand into the bowl filled with what might be blueberries. He munched happily.

"Tell me about the Felcats." Susanna sat back down and sipped more of the beverage.

"They are old." Naomi took a seat. She held her cup tightly in her hands.

"How old?" Kal sat cross-legged on the floor so he could look at them both.

Susanna glanced at the marble deck, her cheeks a bit more warm than normal. She wasn't sure why she felt that way except for the look in Kal's eyes. They reminded her of how Gary had looked at her, full of love.

She felt warm fingers on hers. "By our own beliefs," Naomi said, "he awaits you in the presence of the All Knowing One."

She'd forgotten about the woman being able to read her mind. "True." Her eyes turned to their hostess. "Other than old, what can you tell us about them?"

"They are the historians of the Five Systems and Borders. We suspect of other worlds as well, but we are unsure."

"Do they record the histories?" Kal sipped his beverage and tossed a few more berries into his mouth.

"Not as you would no." Naomi shook her head. "We know only that they meet during the time of the three moons. They share what they know and return to wherever it is they left."

"Nice and vague," Kal huffed.

"They tell us little." She leaned down and placed her cup on the floor.

"Then how do you know they keep the histories?" Kal was reminding Susanna of a stubborn dog who didn't want to release on command.

"Sometimes, Nels thoughts leak into mine." She got up and gazed outside. "Felcats do not think as you and I so it is difficult to understand."

"But you have one with you."

"Even so." She turned to face them. "They seem to like the Rovers and travel with many of us."

Susanna said, "Yet they're not pets."

"No. They are companions."

Kal and Susanna exchanged a look. "Seems God made a complex universe." His works amazed her.

"You can say that again." Kal chuckled. "I wonder what Larry would say to all this?"

She wondered the same thing. "I hope we get to find out." She addressed their hostess. "What's your next stop?"

"We have a trading area where we will meet the Mosi. It is close to your colony."

Probably the one Dr. Byers had found. "Kal and I can probably find our way back from there."

A shadow passed over Naomi's face. One that Susanna couldn't read.

"I am sure." She went to the door. "If you need anything else, messengers of the All Knowing One, we will answer." She pointed to a device on the wall. "You have only to press this and speak." With a whirl of her dark green skirt, the Rover woman was gone.

"You get the impression something is up?" Kal asked.

"Something is." Susanna finished her drink. "How are the berries?"

"Not bad. Taste sort of like a combination of nuts and black cherries."

"Hmmm." She tried a few. They weren't bad and they did seem to fill her stomach. "I really want to get back to Geri."

"And me to Krissy." He picked up their empty mugs, replacing them on the platter. He frowned. "This look familiar to you?"

He ran a finger across it.

Susanna came to stand beside him. Her fingers touched the smooth, warm feeling platter. "Yes."

Kal's expression turned thoughtful. "I wonder."

"Wonder what?" It did seem familiar but Susanna couldn't place it.

"I'd be interested in where they got it." He sprawled out on one of the couches, making sure his cloak covered most of his body. His still slightly muddy boots hung off the end.

It was slightly chilly in the room. She shivered and pulled her cloak more tightly around her.

The door opened again. This time, the cat stood there with one tawny paw pulled tightly against its chest. "Reroow?"

"I have no idea what you just asked," Susanna responded. She heard Kal chuckle as he threw his arm over his eyes.

The Felcat sat down and groomed its chest with a very pink tongue.

"And Naomi said you are intelligent." Somehow the image didn't fit.

Two blue eyes blinked at her. The tail rested casually over the front paws.

Of course, humans were new in space. Maybe what seemed odd to her wasn't all that unusual. Besides, who knew how an intelligent being would act or look?

There was a noise in the hallway. The feline turned its head to look behind it, its ears twitching.

An odd feeling began in Susanna's stomach and she hastily glanced at the open 'window'. The ground below was receding, vanishing into thick rolling clouds.

"We're moving!"

"Huh?" Kal moved his arm and stared at her.

"The ship. We've launched."

"Didn't feel it." He got up and came to stand next to her. "You're right."

"You think I'd make it up," she snapped.

"No."

"Reraaw."

They both fixed their gaze on the cat. It turned and with a flick of its tail, went out the door.

She had a crazy idea. "Let's follow Nels."

Kal grabbed her hand. They left the room and discovered the cat waiting for them on the stairs. It padded up the narrow metal, pausing to make sure they were still there.

Two flights up, it leaped to the deck and confidently trotted to a door. Susanna was curious where the Felcat was taking them.

The door opened and they entered a room that held nothing but an odd globe. Images grew close and faded away inside it. It stood on a narrow base, held in its pace by three cream colored prongs. Axel T'Ganth stood with his fingers lightly resting on the orb.

"I see Nels decided you should see how we control our vessels." His deep voice startled Susanna.

"This is how you fly?" Kal moved past her to walk around the device. "I don't see how you can control it."

"Telepathy, as you would call it, is not uncommon among us."

"I suppose your cousin Hedron is telepathic as well?"

Axel shook his head. "No. Hedron's gifts are different."

The Rovers had a strong sense of what gifts were Susanna reflected as she watched an odd shaped image float to the top of the orb. "What is that?"

"Something that should not be here." Axel's eyes narrowed and the anger in them even she could see.

"Who are they?" She dared to walk closer and stare into the depths.

"Ships of the Aarkon."

"Who's that?"

"He who rules the Five Systems."

Kal finally stopped circling. He too, stared at the image.

The Aarkon's ships were wedge shaped, with long tubs running along the wings. Unlike how they might be shown in an Earth drawing, which would have been bright orange, yellow and blue fire shooting out, there seemed to be shimmering waves escaping instead.

Fear for the colony and everyone she loved filled Susanna. "Is the Aarkon a good or bad ruler?"

Nels hissed.

"Depends on the man." Axel must have adjusted something because the ships vanished. They were replaced by a rocky landing field and a primitive structure. Damp drizzle dripped down the logs and Susanna could see thick mud below them.

Kal asked, "Your ship doesn't sink in the mud?"

"No. We have an energy field that suspends us just above the ground."

"Convenient."

The ground grew closer and closer until the ship rested about a foot above the mud. Susanna could see bright clear bands vibrating between the vessel and wet soil. What technology they had! How she wished they'd had this when they'd landed here!

"What happens now?" Kal's fingers lightly touched the now quiet orb.

"We wait for the Mosi," Axel replied.

Chapter 23

Shades of purple and pink rippled the wispy clouds. Larry locked his fingers behind his head and gazed with awe at God's finger painting. The rain had finally cleared and faint sunlight touched the sky. Drops glistened on branches reminding him of a lighted Christmas tree.

He cautiously stretched. The branch he rested on swayed slightly. Thankfully, there were no ominous cracks. Leli poked his ginger head out and lazily arched his back, his front legs extended as far as he could reach.

"Good morning to you too," Larry good naturedly told the cat. He stroked Leli's head and turned to see who else was up.

He smiled at the picture in the branch next to him. Jeanie was fast asleep with her head against Jack's shoulder. That caused Larry to frown. The young man had been on the branch above him last night. At some point the soldier must have descended without disturbing anyone. T was cradled against the pair. The dog whined and wagged his tail.

Larry glanced up and grinned at the young Mosi curled tightly into a ball. She was resting comfortably like she had done this her entire life. No doubt she probably had, he reflected.

Yoana dropped onto his branch and he grabbed at the trunk. The branch shook up and down under the older Mosi's weight.

"Morning," Larry greeted.

She tipped her head to the side and he got a glimpse of the sharp teeth as she ran her dark red tongue over them. Yoana reached up and shook an upper branch, dripping the moisture into her mouth.

"Good." Yoana then dropped down to the ground. She shook her body and yowled loudly.

Other bodies slowly moved and eventually joined her.

"Think that's our cue," Larry muttered. He glanced over at Jeanie and Jack. They were awake and kissed each other before Malia helped them get T out of the tree. The three clumsily shimmed down. Leli rode on his shoulders, sharp little claws embedded in his cloak and sometimes his skin. "Ouch," he grumbled, glad to have ground under his feet again after a night in the trees.

Several of the Mosi sniffed and then padded off into the thick trees. It was like giant waves swallowed them up.

"Where are they going?" Larry asked.

"Hunting." Yoana scratched the tree bark. Several long gashes appeared. Yellowish sap oozed from the wound. "Now ours."

Vaguely Larry recalled cats left scratches to mark their territory. Most humans mistakenly thought it was to sharpen their claws. He'd seen Leli do that too both on the carpeted cat trees and sometimes, when the feline didn't think anyone was looking, the back of his mother's couch.

He took a quick breath. The pain of leaving his parents behind, while beginning to fade, still could jab his heart.

"So now what?" Jeanie stood beside him. She shook her cloak out. Water sprayed everywhere.

T decided it was a good idea too and shook his body. The trio put up their hands to try and protect themselves.

Malia and Yoana snarled.

"It's what dogs do," Larry explained. His gaze then drifted to Jack. The young soldier was alert, watching all around them, his hand hovering above his weapon.

"Trouble?" Larry tensed.

Jack shook his head. "Not exactly." He pulled out the radio and tried again. "Lewis to base, Lewis to base, anyone copy?" Static hissed in response. The soldier made a face. "We should be close enough for them to hear us."

"You worry too much," Jeanie told him. She tucked her arm around Jack's. "They're probably just playing cards."

"Doubt it." Jack planted a kiss on her forehead. "We've been out of contact for a couple of days. The General should have search parties out."

Silently Larry agreed. He knew military procedure. Why did he have the gut feeling something was very, very wrong?

"Come!" Yoana ordered. She trotted off into the trees.

Malia followed with the dog leash in her hand. T wagged his tail and willingly went with the young Mosi.

"Hope she doesn't think she gets to keep the dog," Jack commented as he took Jeanie's hand.

Larry chuckled as the three headed in the same direction as

the Mosi. Leli curled into the hollow of his arm and seemed to be content staring out at the wet world, protected by his cloak.

The trees seemed to be endless as did the slick mud under his boots. Water sometimes dripped down until he finally pulled his hood up to protect his head. He noticed Jeanie did the same thing.

What seemed like hours later, they finally emerged into a damp and sweet smelling field. Almost, it was as if they stood in a field of wheat after a spring rain. However, the odor had a bit more of a bitter tinge.

Larry wrinkled his nose. "Ugh."

"Ah, it's not that bad," Jeanie smirked back.

"Speak for yourself, little sister."

She straightened self-importantly. "I was."

"Now just what," Jack pointed at an ugly large gray-green splotch, "is that?"

"The traders," Malia explained. She put her paws behind her back, T's leash draped over them.

"They come here often?" Larry couldn't wait to tell Susanna, that is, if they'd been found. *Please, God, tell me they're safe and back at the colony!*

"Two, maybe three times. Always in the seasons of wet or hot."

He noticed the absence of a cold season. So, the traders didn't come then. Larry found himself speculating on where the Mosi spent the winter.

"Where do you go in the time of cold?" he asked Malia.

She blinked her round yellow-gold eyes. "Where you found us."

Made sense. Caves held a constant temperature. "You will return there after you meet with the traders?"

"Depends on Yoana." She hurried over to the Mosi leader. The tribe was standing together, staring across the large field, yet not moving toward the traders' ship.

"I think there's a problem." Jack's hand again hovered near his pistol.

His youngest sister stared up into the soldier's face. "What makes you say that?"

He pointed with his chin. "Look."

All around the orb ship were some dark human like shapes, not to mention vessels reminding Larry of the Stealth bombers used in the late part of the Twentieth Century.

"More unwelcomed company you think?" Larry put his hand on Jeanie's damp shoulder.

"Yeah." Jack pursed his lips.

Leli urped and put out a paw. It rested on Larry's arm.

Yoana padded back to them. She snarled. "You bring trouble."

"We brought trouble?" Jack shot back. "I don't see any of us over there."

"Then you no see. Blind like those just born."

Larry put out a staying hand when he saw Jack was about to retort. "Our eyes can't see what you do."

Jack glared at Larry and narrowed his eyes.

Malia glided up. "Human female, like you yet not, with the soldiers of the Aarkon."

He suddenly needed to see. Larry turned to Yoana. "Can you get us close without being seen?"

Her head swiveled around on her short neck. She gazed at the distant threat. "Maybe already too late."

"Or maybe not." Larry prayed the alien soldiers couldn't see them any clearer than he could see the potential enemy.

"Maybe he right." Malia handed T's leash over to Jeanie. "They no see human female."

The Mosi leader made a type of hissing sound. "We go back to the trees." She was gone with a flick of her long spotted tail.

"Jeanie, you go with them," Larry instructed his sister.

"Now you wait just a minute,"

"You're Your brother is right," Jack interrupted her before she went off on a tirade.

"Here." Larry handed over Leli. His sister awkwardly took the cat while juggling the leash with her other hand.

"What did I say about you men trying to protect little ole me?"

"Go!" Jack ordered with a slap on Jeanie's butt.

"Ouch!" She glared at the soldier. "You're gonna pay for that!"

"So what. Now get!" The younger man pointed to the safety of the forest.

"Oh, all right." She grumbled under her breath as she marched back into the trees.

"Yoana protect. You no worry." Malia headed toward the forest edge. She stopped when she realized neither man had moved. "Come!"

"Trusting our lives to an over grown cat," Jack complained.

"An ally," Larry corrected.

They took off at a run and loped with the Mosi along the forest edge. She led them across a swollen chilly stream and Larry groaned. It was cold enough without adding cold feet to the formula.

Malia then slipped and slid up a muddy hill and plopped down behind some spiky magenta bushes. Larry kneeled beside her, trying to ignore the grime on the hem of his cloak. Jack peered through and whistled.

"That's Dragoon!"

"You sure?" Larry squinted and finally made out the dark haired woman standing next to a soldier in an odd red uniform. It fitted tightly to the man's body almost like a jumpsuit only in two pieces. There was some sort of white braid on his shoulder.

"Spent too much time around her not to know her by sight."

"See the general anywhere?"

Jack shook his head. "General Borromeo warned most of us there could be trouble, but he never specified what kind."

Larry remembered the warning over the radio a couple of days ago. None of the soldiers were to listen to Dragoon if she ordered a return to base.

"What else did he tell you?" Larry almost resented the General keeping a secret. He'd counted the man among his allies in the colony.

"Only to be ready for trouble." Jack glanced at Larry. "You know there's been problems between him and Dragoon."

"I think the whole colony must have known."

"Naw, not everyone. Most are too blind. They wanted to think we were all one big happy family."

Experience told Larry Jack was probably right. Most would have ignored the subtle signs of trouble between the two leaders. The colonists were looking to start over and live better than they could have back on a ruined Earth.

Jack pulled a small pair of binoculars out of his pocket. He put them against his eyes and looked out on the scene.

"What do you see?" Larry wanted to know.

"Dragoon and the soldier, whom I'm guessing is the commanding officer, are talking."

"But Borromeo isn't there." Larry wanted to confirm that point.

"The General isn't. Wait a sec," Jack leaned forward. "Some sort of hatch just opened on the trader's ship."

Larry wished he could see better. "And?"

"And there are some figures coming out."

"How many?"

"One, two, three, four."

Malia said, "The traders."

"Yeah, maybe." Something in Jack's voice made Larry uncertain about what the Mosi saw.

"Jack?"

"It's Susanna and Kal!" Jack pulled back and grinned.

"With the traders?" Larry really wished he could see what the other had.

"Here." The soldier pushed the binoculars at Larry.

He took them and found a clear spot through the thorns. Sure enough, Susanna and Kal were standing next to another man and woman although they were dressed in the same dark green clothes as the traders.

"Thank you, Lord," Larry breathed. "Can't wait to hear their story!"

"Makes two of us." Jack extended his hand for the binoculars. Larry handed them back. "Wish I could read lips."

"The Captain is saying," Malia said. "That they always come here to trade."

The Aarkon commander or else Dragoon must have asked what the traders were doing there.

"Female you call Dragoon is saying how he shouldn't be here. This planet now hers." Malia snarled and hissed.

"We didn't know you were here," Larry said.

"You God's messengers." Her ears twitched forward. "We expected you."

Larry still wasn't sure what to make of that revelation. He knew one day God would supply all the answers. He just hoped he learned them during his lifetime and didn't have to wait until he got to heaven.

"Dragoon demanding the trader captain turn over the two

others. He refused. Said they are guests. Protected under Rover hos…pi…ta..li..ty." Malia had problems saying the last word.

"We need to get down there," Jack said. The younger man replaced the binoculars and reached for his weapon.

"Don't," Larry warned. The holy spirit told him it would be a mistake to go in with a gun brandished.

"It's the only advantage we have!"

Larry grinned and shook his head. He understood Jack's confusion. There was no way to explain to him God had appointed this moment and had everything under control.

"Just follow me, Jack. Malia, stay here. If we're captured, I want you to make sure Jeanie, Leli and T are safe. Can you do that for me?"

"Yes." The young Mosi was confused, but he sensed she'd obey.

"No gun." Larry wanted Jack to listen. It was important.

Resigned the soldier replied, "Whatever."

The two went back down the slippery hill and walked around it. Larry trudged through the muck until he could be seen by the Aarkon soldiers. Several hands were raised and he wasn't sure if it was in greeting or a type of weapon he didn't know about.

Dragoon stepped forward, her hands resting on her hips. "Where did you come from?"

Chapter 24

Two figures emerged from behind a hill and Susanna wanted to shout a warning.

Her brother stopped near the soldiers who had raised hands. Slowly his arms went up, his palms open showing he was unarmed. Jack did the same, although she doubted the younger man had left his gun behind. It was probably under his coat.

"Cirz," Naomi said.

"Excuse me?" Susanna had no idea what the other woman was talking about.

"They're weapons and sit in the hand like so." She demonstrated by cupping her own. A small circular device rested in her palm. It was sliver with a red crystal in the middle. Susanna had no idea how it was operated because there weren't any controls.

"Explains their posture." Kal slid an arm around Susanna's waist. She wasn't sure if it was for comfort or a protective move.

"Deadly?" Susanna was afraid for Larry and Jack.

Naomi shook her head. "Rarely."

Axel moved forward to place himself between the party on the ramp and the Aarkon's men. "Why are you here?" he demanded.

"They're here at my request." Dragoon glared at him. Susanna had to admit she looked formidable in her dark cloak despite her small stature.

"That much was obvious." The Rover's tone was almost dismissive.

"We've had a long standing," Dragoon stopped as if she suddenly realized she'd said too much.

Naomi went to her husband and whispered in his ear. His eyes narrowed. Susanna wondered what his wife had said to him.

"You've had a long standing what?" Larry barked. He moved forward ignoring the cirz all centered on him. "What secrets have you been keeping and where's General Borromeo?"

"Under house arrest," she snapped back. "Just as all of you will be."

"For what reason?"

"Do you have any idea how long you've been out of contact?" Dragoon smiled, but it wasn't one of greeting, rather, Susanna reflected, like a won battle.

Jack spoke up. "Radio didn't work."

"Likely excuse." Their leader turned to the Aarkon commander. "Take them back to the colony. My aids will show you where to lock them up."

Susanna saw the restless shifting among the soldiers. Their glances became nervous as if some sort of danger approached.

"Hold your ground!" their commander ordered.

With a gasp Susanna saw several leopard people join Larry and Jack. With them was Jeanie. On her sister's shoulder rode Leli and behind her the Husky Susanna remembered from the bus. Now why in the world did they have the dog?

Kal leaned toward her. "Reminds me of those cowboy and Indian movies where the bad guys suddenly find themselves surrounded."

She nodded, her golden-brown eyes darting around to see if what Kal said might be the truth.

"It's you," Axel continued as he stood his ground, "who do not belong here."

"It's our planet," Dragoon spat back.

"No," one of the leopards pushed her way forward. "It's our world."

"She's correct." Axel's gaze rested on the Aarkon commander who uneasily shifted from one booted foot to the other.

Glancing from one man to the other, Susanna sensed something important was about to happen. "Pray," she said quietly to Kal.

"What?"

"Pray." He tightened his hold on her and she saw his eyes half close.

Oh, Father! Susanna didn't know what else to say. She understood that sometimes lengthy prayers weren't needed. So much could be said in just a few words with tons of emotion behind them.

"He's got a point." Larry came to stand next to the leopard female. "This planet doesn't belong to us, Dragoon. The Mosi were here before us."

"Animals," she sneered.

The Aarkon commander corrected her, "Intelligent beings. The Charon are recognized as such under the covenant contracts."

Dragoon spun around, her fingers hooked as if she might rent him to pieces with her nails. "The what?"

Susanna heard Axel chuckle. "You weren't told were you?"

"We were guaranteed a habitable planet to colonize!" The oriental woman had an almost wild, desperate look on her face.

"That can still be granted." Axel held the eyes of the Aarkon Commander. "Is that not so?" Susanna wondered if he was telepathically controlling the other.

Reluctantly the other nodded. "Yes."

"But we surveyed this world!" Dragoon frantically glanced between the two men. Susanna suspected control of the situation had just been taken away from the colony's leader.

"Hastily I would say." Axel pinned Dragoon with a hard stare. The woman blanched and looked at the ground.

"There was a lot missing we didn't know," Susanna dared to interject.

"And needless deaths," Naomi added. "Is that not so Lin Dragoon?"

The small body of their leader shook and almost seemed to shrivel. "Yes."

"What do you mean?" Kal demanded.

Naomi gave him a sad look. "It is not for me to say. Only that one," she pointed at Dragoon, "can tell you the truth."

Kal pulled away from Susanna and stalked down the ramp. His boots sloshed in the mud and he stood before Dragoon. He demanded. "What is she talking about?"

Part of Susanna suspected he already knew the truth. *Did Dragoon kill his sister?* she asked God.

Dragoon fell to her knees, her eyes closed. "Your sister knew too much."

"About what?" Susanna could see Kal shaking. She just hoped he didn't try to hurt a woman who was already defeated.

"About the agreement."

"Ahhhh!" He raised his foot as if to kick her. Larry hurried over and put a staying hand on the other man's shoulder.

"What agreement?" Larry took over the questioning.

Dragoon refused to answer. Naomi and her husband exchanged a glance. He nodded. The Rover woman spoke quietly, "If you do not willingly speak, I will force you to."

Her words caused a slight shiver to run down Susanna's spine. She knew Naomi could read minds. What else might she or Axel be able to do?

"I will do you great harm if I am forced to do what must be done." The warning in Naomi's voice was clear.

"She knew about the agreement." Dragoon didn't raise her eyes. "Earth contacted the Aarkon years ago."

There were gasps all around and some snarls from the Mosi, as her brother and Axel had called them.

"It was he who gave us the technology to advance our ships and often supplied possible planets for us to colonize."

No wonder the platter had seemed familiar! Susanna realized. It was like the outside of the *Namid*.

"Made a bad choice with this one," Larry said.

"The survey was incomplete because of the need to hurry. Our time had run out."

"Why kill my sister?" Kal asked.

"Because she would have told your president and he did not know." Dragoon finally lifted her hate filled eyes to glare at Kal and Larry. Susanna hugged herself. She wouldn't have wanted to have that look leveled at her.

"So *you* killed her." Larry rubbed his jaw. "The General thought the president ordered it."

The colony leader huffed. "I let him believe that."

"What else have you been hiding?" Jack stepped over. Susanna noticed his hand hovered over where his gun must be hidden.

"You're just a child." Dragoon slowly got to her feet. "You," she spun to face Susanna, "weren't supposed to come."

Startled, she could just stare at the other woman. "Excuse me?"

"Your husband."

It was as if someone poked a sharp stick into her heart. She knew the truth but was afraid to acknowledge it.

"We killed him hoping you would not come. I had someone else I wanted to lead the scientists. Instead," she hissed, "you came and brought them!" She pointed first at Larry and then Jeanie.

A hand flung out, striking their leader and knocking her to

the ground. Everyone stared in shock at the Aarkon commander.

"Murderer!" He snapped his fingers and two soldiers stepped forward. "Secure her in my ship. She will answer directly to the Aarkon."

They grabbed her under her arms and took her away, dragging her cloak through the thick mud.

The commander turned to the Rover captain. "You are correct this world belongs to the Charon. My ships will remove the offensive colony."

"But not the messengers," the leopard female Susanna suspected might be the matriarch stepped forward. "They may stay."

"Messengers?" The commander looked to the Rover to explain.

"They're the ones the Charon and Rovers have been waiting for." Axel said nothing else. The commander only shook his head. He obviously had no idea what the Rover was talking about.

The commander snapped orders and led his men toward the colony.

"What does he mean by removing them?" Larry asked.

Axel pointed with his chin. "The colonists will be relocated to another world along with whatever structures have been set up."

"Not the messengers!" the female hissed.

"Relax, Yoana." Axel smiled at her.

Susanna finally relaxed enough to rush down the ramp and embrace her brother. He returned the hug. "Good to see you, too."

Jeanie hugged her too. Leli's whiskers tickled Susanna's face.

"Whatever are you doing out here with the cat?"

"Oh, Leli invited himself along." Jeanie reached up and scratched his head.

"Okay." Susanna suspected there was more to the story yet it would probably be several days before she heard it all.

"What will they do to Dragoon?" Larry asked the Rover captain.

"It depends on the Aarkon's mood and what other offenses the commander brings to his attention." Axel shrugged. "It hardly matters since her fate is not something for you to worry about."

"But the General's is." Jack turned and headed for the colony.

"Think I'll go with him and keep him out of trouble." Jeanie hurried after the soldier. Leli protested and the dog obediently trotted behind.

"I proposed to your sister," Kal told Larry. Susanna felt her face grow hot.

"She answer?" Larry seemed unconcerned.

"Not yet."

"Hmmm. Need me to talk to her?"

"Naw. I'm willing to wait."

"Would you two stop talking about me like I'm not here?" She put her hands on her hips and glared at them.

They both smiled.

"Gladly, sis."

~ * ~

Three days later the entire colony had been dismantled and loaded into the cargo bays of the military ships. Ninety-nine percent of the colonists decided to relocate to Res. It was in the neighboring system and had a tropical climate. Susanna would bet they were tired of the cold and rain.

One of Dragoon's assistants, Trace Lee, proved to be an excellent leader; cooperating with the Aakon's men and helping people pack to relocate. He was voted in unanimously to take over when they reached Res.

Susanna stood with her family on the edge of the field watching as the last of the colonists boarded the Aarkon ships.

Larry shook his head. "I was really hoping the colony wouldn't divide."

"Not your fault, son." Borromeo clapped a fatherly hand on her brother's shoulder.

"Messengers," Jack snorted.

"You can still leave," Jeanie replied, although her face said otherwise.

"Naw." He winked at her. "I don't think you'd survive one night on your own if I did."

"Ha!"

Kal was holding Krissy and Susanna once more had her daughter in her arms. The baby gurgled happily. She glanced at her brother as Amira Upala began to get on the ship. "Larry," she took a deep breath. "If you let that woman go, it'll be the biggest mistake of your life."

"You heard her the other night at dinner. She's feels responsible for everyone. It's her duty to go."

"But not I think what her heart wants." She hadn't missed the way the doctor kept looking at her brother. Amira was in love with him. Larry was just too stupid to realize it.

Larry munched on his lower lip. She knew the conflict he was feeling. He would never go against Amira's wishes.

She finally pushed. "What did God say?"

He threw her a startled look before dashing across the field and grabbing the doctor. By their expressions there she was sure some heated words were being exchanged. Amira turned to go again and he grabbed her arm.

She whirled on him and he kissed her. The look on Amira's face was priceless. She took a step back and then kissed him back. Hard.

Kal chuckled. "I think the matter is settled."

Susanna smiled in agreement.

Chapter 25

The few who stayed behind sat in a circle around the fire. The Mosi had gone to gather the other Charon. Larry knew it was time for all twenty-four of them to make a hard decision. The Rover ship still sat where it had landed. Her crew safely inside for the night.

"So," Borromeo inquired, "What is this decision you think we should all make? Seems, son, we've already made it."

Larry was prepared for the argument. God had put this on his heart and he knew he had to share it. "Remember how the Rovers said this world belongs to the Charon?"

Everyone nodded. Although most hadn't actually physically been there at the time, he knew the story had been spread.

"Well," he shifted his legs into a more comfortable position. The ground was hard and damp, despite the grass he'd spread there. "I agree. This planet is theirs and despite the fact they don't mind if the messengers stay behind, somehow, it doesn't seem right."

Susanna spoke up. "You're thinking along the lines of the missionaries who went to the American Indians and did damage to their culture by forcing their morals upon them instead of allowing them to keep their traditions and way of life."

"Something like that." He raised a hand at the murmuring. "I know, I know. We think we have learned from past mistakes."

Borromeo agreed. "I think Pastor Larry has a point. We'd do more damage than good."

"But they want to learn about God!" someone objected.

"They did ask us to stay," Jack reminded him.

"They did yes, but we all know human nature even if we're almost all Christians."

Amira nodded her agreement. He reached over and took her hand. She wasn't ready to accept Christ yet. She had an open mind though and that was all Larry was asking.

Larry raised his voice over the grumbling. "What I propose is that we ask the Rovers to take us off this planet."

"Why didn't we just go with the others?" Joyce, the pediatric nurse asked.

"Would you have?" Trish O'Malley asked. "Seems to me we got the better deal. I think we should listen to Larry here."

Larry's heart began to drum in his chest. "I talked with Axel earlier today." He knew many wouldn't like what he was about to say. He'd preplanned their removal without talking to everyone first. "There are three more clan ships on their way here."

Silence met his announcement.

"Each is from a different clan." Axel had explained how they *all* wanted to hear about the Son of the All Knowing One.

"So," Jack poked at the fire. It crackled breaking some of the building tension. "Our small group is going to be separated again."

"Wasn't really my call." Larry understood what Jack meant. Separations were going to be hard. "But God gave us all one ministry—to spread His good news."

He had to wait for the realization to set in. Slowly, across all their faces he saw the dawning and understanding looks in their eyes.

"We're not going to pull families apart. In fact," he chuckled, "Axel told me the clans are a big extended family with some related by blood and others not."

It had been a fascinating discussion. Larry couldn't wait to learn more about the Rovers and live among them.

"Like God's family," Jeanie said. She leaned against Jack who put his arm around her. They looked so right together and Larry hoped the young man found his way to Christ. He would be a good husband for her.

Larry took a deep breath. "What everyone needs to decide is—which of you want to go together and to what clan."

"And the clans are, son?" Borromeo asked.

"The T'Ganth's, Vi'anth's, the Wayas and the Talons."

He overhead Kal say to Susanna, "They only told us about three. Interesting."

"They named three but said there were others." His sister pulled her cloak over Geri. The night air was getting chilly. Krissy snuggled against Susanna and she kissed the toddlers head. Those four were already a family.

"I don't have a ton of information on the clans," Larry continued. "From what I gather they're all pretty much the same just on different planets. However, they're settled in an area they call the Borders. It isn't part of the Five Systems."

"Sounds ominous," Jeanie said, with a huge grin on her face. "Like we're going to be on the edge of the galaxy."

Oddly enough, there was a lot of truth to what she had just said. Still, Larry knew the Rovers traded with the Five Systems and other planets Axel hadn't been willing to talk about. Maybe some of them included lost Earth colonies or maybe those intelligent dragons Kal had mentioned once.

"What was it the Bible said, Jeanie?" Larry loved pulling scripture out. "How the word of God was going to spread all over the world."

"Not out here though," Kal said. "Funny that."

"Maybe it was part of the Bible Code," Jeanie suggested, "and we don't know about it because we never asked."

Something fluttered across Amira's face. Larry turned to her. He didn't know exactly what to ask.

She sighed. "It does say in the Bible Code as you call it, that God's word will spread among the stars. We just didn't believe it."

Wow! Larry was stunned. He was sure everyone else was as well. "Surprised you hadn't said something before."

She shrugged. "I didn't think it was important and wasn't sure if I should believe it either."

"Do you now?" Larry waited for her answer.

Hesitantly she answered, "Yes."

He squeezed her fingers and turned his attention back to the main group. "I hope we're all in agreement that we should relocate and leave the planet to its rightful owners the Charon."

Slowly everyone nodded. Larry smiled. He knew in his heart it was the right decision and was glad the other Christians had realized it too.

~ * ~

Days later they were once again on the field with four ugly, splotched orbs, hovering over the muddy ground. The Charon had gathered as well and were not too happy about God's messengers leaving.

Larry understood their feelings but knew staying would damage their culture to a point beyond repair. That had happened with many primitive people back on Earth. The mistake did not need to be repeated here. At least the Christians could start their new lives the right way on the various Homefalls.

Susanna and Kal were saying good-bye to Axel, Naomi and Hedron. Their ship was the largest and a group of ten wanted to stay together. The colonists had already boarded and no doubt were settling in for the trip. There was a couple who were going with the Wayas and three single women, including Trish and Joyce who had opted to accompany the Vi'anths.

Larry, Amira, Kal, Krissy, Susanna, Geri, Jack and Jeanie, had decided, after praying together about it, to go with the Talons.

"Thank you again," Susanna said as she hugged Naomi.

"It was our great pleasure." The Rover woman wiped a tear from her eye.

Kal waved as he and Susanna re-joined them.

In silence they watched the hatch close. The orb gently lifted into the sky and vanished. It was followed by the ships of the Wayas and Vi'anths.

"Well," Kal said, putting his arm around Susanna, "never thought about being a missionary, but I guess God had other plans."

"He always does," Susanna answered. She stared lovingly at her baby she held. "And by the way," She eyes raised to meet Kal's. "Yes, I will marry you."

"About time." Kal grinned and kissed Larry's sister, being careful not to squish Geri. Krissy hung onto her uncle's pants smiling.

Jeanie rolled her eyes. "So slow."

"You're next," Jack shot back.

"Oh? I believe there's a little matter of you accepting Christ first."

"Really?" Larry didn't miss the teasing look in the younger man's eyes. "And just what makes you think I'm even interested?"

She punched Jack's arm and bent down to pick up Leli. "We have the entire voyage to the Talon Homefall to discuss it." Jeanie hooked her arm around the soldier's. "Let's go find a bunk before the *old* people beat us to the best ones."

"Thanks a lot," Larry bantered back.

"Any time, big brother."

The young couple and cat rushed across the field and board-ed the ship. Susanna handed Geri to Kal and took Krissy's hand.

The new family headed for the green-orange orb.

"I'll meet you on the ship." Amira paused. "The voyage should give us time to talk of this Jesus I've heard so much about."

"I won't push you to make a decision."

"As I have said, you are most unusual pastor." She trailed after the others to the Talons' ship.

Larry took a moment to look once more at the planet that had briefly been their home. Odd colors of yellow and deep blue patterned the horizon. He found himself ready to move on and discover what the Talon Homefall was like. Would it be alien or welcoming?

"Best get going, son." Borromeo extended a hand. Larry shook it.

"You don't have to stay here alone."

"I'm not." The General smiled, the light reflecting off his white teeth. "God is with me. Besides, I think the Charon would have kept someone captive if at least one of us hadn't agreed to stay."

"Maybe." Borromeo might have been right.

Yoana came to claim their messenger. "Good voyage."

"God bless." Larry heard her faint purr. She must have liked the blessing.

He tipped his head to the general and went to board the ship. The Talon captain waited by the hatch and closed it after Larry.

"Welcome aboard, messenger of the All Knowing One," the captain greeted. "The rest of the clan are excited you are coming. We have waited a long, long time to hear of the All Knowing One's son."

About the Author

Dana Bell enjoys writing regional tales and has lived many places including Boston, MA., Idaho and Oregon. Currently residing in Colorado, many of her stories are set there and star the various cats she is and has been owned by. She enjoys constructing and decorating dollhouses, all of which have rich background on the inhabitants. She's also a talented editor and enjoys helping other authors improve their craft and succeed.

Other Books by Dana Bell from Wolf Singer Publications

Winter Awakening

In a world of snow and biting wind, two enemies must decide if they can trust each other enough to find out the truth of their changing world or if old predator-prey rules remain with no hope for change.

Time Travelling Coffers—edited by Dana Bell

Sit back and be intrigued by stories about a sleigh driven by Santa, a pocket watch given to a friend, an Egyptian box found on another planet, an eternal ring, a supercollider and many other everyday objects. Each of them result in an unexpected journey in time and space.

Different Dragons—edited by Dana Bell

Dragons trapped on a spaceship, awaiting rescue from a human they raised as their own. Ancient reptiles escaped the great flood via a portal and now wish to return.In the desert a dragon lures children, animals and adults to its lair, and only a brave dog can rescue them. A dragon arises in China and seeks to keep its hoard, while two con men try to steal it. Searching for his father, a young man solves an ancient riddle and discovers an awful dragon truth. Nanites, demons, and other mythical creatures join or battle the dracos, as do the humans who encounter them.

These and other tales await within these pages, because here—be *Different Dragons*.

More mind bending Science Fiction from WolfSinger Publications

Aqua Vitae—Therese Arkenberg

Jenes Inarya wants to experience everything. And quite frankly, she doesn't think she can live life to the fullest in the time she's been allotted. A search through lore and legend from the Eight Immortals of Chinese myth to the Garden of Eden finally leads her to what she seeks--across the galaxy, to the planet of Arak, which possesses an immortal ecosystem. By eating food prepared from the immortal plants of Arak, Jenes can alter her metabolism and gain eternal life. In her case, it's a cup of palm wine. A real aqua vitae.

But the prospect of eternal life quickly causes more problems than it solves.

Claire—Sally Kuntz

It was an open and shut case of someone's reckless actions that had killed his sister. Mark knows that, and he is going to expose the group responsible for the wild, headlong, daredevils they are. But Mark has a lot to learn; about the killer and about himself.

Mark arrives on Eire's moon with a complete set of beliefs: it hadn't been his sister's fault in any way, the person responsible for shooting down his sister's ship, the group the killer belongs to are reckless scum, and he will right the situation by exposing them in print. But the longer he stays the less his beliefs apply.

Remember Me to Paradise—Amy Benesch

A Shapeshifter from a planet known as Paradise, comes to Earth on a mission to rescue other Shapeshifters who may have become trapped in Earth shapes and are unable to return to their home planet.

During his time on Earth the Shapeshifter becomes a dog, a duck, a pigeon, a human male, and a human female. It is as a human female that Shapeshifter begins to forget its true identity. She goes to a therapist who urges her to write down her dreams.

Although her dreams terrify her (she can't understand why she dreams of flying and of making love to women), she keeps working to put the pieces of the puzzle together and recover her memory, although with each passing day she becomes more identified with her current shape and less likely to believe the truth of who she really is.

Schrodinger's Cat—Eileen Schuh

Chordelia, straddling two of the realities proposed in Everett's Many Worlds Theory of Quantum Physics, has no idea how distorted the line is between choice and fate.

In one of her worlds, Chorie's young daughter is dying—a drama that quickly contaminates her other, much rosier, reality. Before long, the emotional burden of dealing with two separate lives spawns heated legal battles, endangers her role as mother and wife, and causes people in both universes to judge her insane. As her lives begin to crumble, so does Chorie's heart and mind.

When Dr. Penny, a man with disturbing, murky, hypnotic eyes offers to rid her of the life that's causing so much pain, she must decide if she is willing to sacrifice the chance to be with her dying child for the chance to save her marriage and experience happiness.

She thinks she's planned it well—she's researched her choices, prepared herself for the consequences, put everything in place. She makes her decision. However....

Life, as it has the propensity to do, strikes back with the dark and unexpected.

Check them out at www.wolfsingerpubs.com